THE GRIZZLY ROSE TO ITS HIND LEGS . . .

With yellow fangs snapping, it charged . . . There was no escape to the rear, so Chance took the only path open to him—he ran directly at the beast. His hope was that the animal would be so startled it would retreat and give him the opportunity to dive for his fallen rifle. That hope died at the end of a clawed paw that slammed directly into the center of Chance's chest. The bear's brute strength lifted Chance from his feet and hurled him through the air. But there was no hillside to halt his flight. There was nothing but empty space as the gambler was flung over the two-hundred-foot drop . . .

Other Exciting Westerns in Avon Books'
CHANCE Series

CHANCE
(#2) RIVERBOAT RAMPAGE
(#3) DEAD MAN'S HAND
(#4) GAMBLER'S REVENGE
(#5) DELTA RAIDERS
(#6) MISSISSIPPI ROGUE

Coming Soon

(#8) MISSOURI MASSACRE

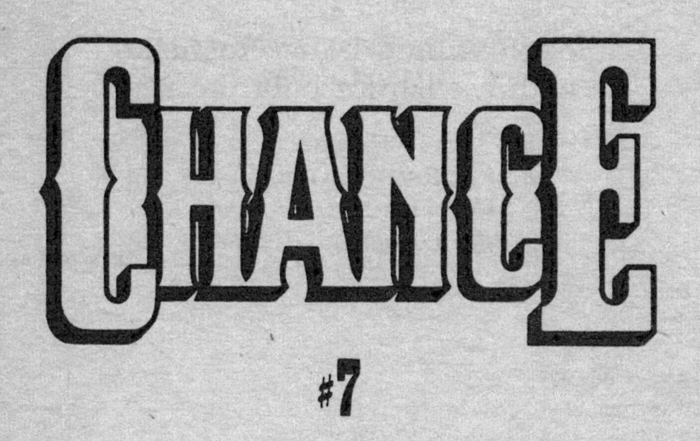

#7

DAKOTA SHOWDOWN

CLAY TANNER

AVON
PUBLISHERS OF BARD, CAMELOT, DISCUS AND FLARE BOOKS

For John and Diane Rochelle—
with a wish for only the best

CHANCE #7: DAKOTA SHOWDOWN is an original publication of Avon Books. This work has never before appeared in book form.

AVON BOOKS
A division of
The Hearst Corporation
105 Madison Avenue
New York, New York 10016

Published by arrangement with the author
Library of Congress Catalog Card Number: 87-91171
ISBN: 0-380-75392-8

First Avon Printing: September 1987

AVON TRADEMARK REG. U.S. PAT. OFF. AND IN OTHER COUNTRIES, MARCA REGISTRADA, HECHO EN U.S.A.

Printed in the U.S.A.

K-R 10 9 8 7 6 5 4 3 2 1

ONE

Decay hung in the air. The sickeningly sweet smell of putrid flesh floated just beneath the disguising rich aroma of coffee beans, a dusty trace of flour, a spicy hint of peppers, and the tempting tartness of dried apples. Through this mélange of odors Captain Bert Rooker led the riverboat gambler Chance Sharpe.

"You smell it, don't you?" Captain Rooker's dark eyes darted to his companion.

"A hint," Chance agreed, then motioned the square-built man deeper into the dimly lit supply room.

The black-suited gambler barely kept his irritation in check as he followed the captain toward three barrels near the back of the room. Although he did not deny the deep personal satisfaction that stemmed from his ownership of the elegant side-wheeler the *Wild Card,* sometimes the mundane responsibility required of a riverboat proprietor seemed to outweigh the pleasures. After all, a gambler was meant to ply his trade at the green-felt–covered gaming tables and not in a ship's pantry.

"The chef found 'em not more than fifteen minutes ago and came right to me." Bert Rooker's gravelly voice contained a touch of irritation of its own. "Should have double-checked these before we pulled out of Fort Buford!"

Chance wasn't certain who Bert indicted for not checking the supplies. Less than a year had passed since the gambler had won the *Wild Card* in a poker game. The ins and outs of exactly what was expected of him remained a vague gray in certain areas. If he had somehow overlooked one of the numerous duties of a paddlewheeler owner, he was certain the captain would not hesitate to set him straight on the matter. No one had ever accused Captain Bert Rooker of being shy and retiring.

Another man might have found Bert's blustery and overbearing manner offensive. Not so with Chance Sharpe; in their months together aboard the steamer, the gambler had come to respect the captain's experience-tempered opinions and value him as a loyal friend. Even with a foul temper and mouth to match, Chance wouldn't have traded the man for any other captain on the river.

Standing at five foot eight, Bert Rooker was all riverman, suckled at the breasts of the nation's mightiest rivers, the Missouri, Ohio, and Mississippi. All his life Bert had faced the challenge of the river's current, refusing to back down or be broken by its constant dangers. It was a life that forged a backbone of steel and a body as solid as granite. When it came to a fight, there was no better man to have at one's side or back.

Bert reached the first hogshead, lifted the lid, and tossed it aside. The tops of the remaining two barrels were discarded with equal ease. The effluvium of rotting meat filled Chance's nostrils. His head jerked back, and his stomach churned from the overwhelming stench.

"A mite ripe, ain't it?" Amusement laced Bert's tone at Chance's reaction. "One dried beef and two salt pork—they were all sealed tight until the chef opened 'em. That's why they weren't noticed before now."

Chance looked back at the barrels. "A mite ripe" was an understatement. One hogshead of salt pork was crawling with maggots!

"What about our other meat supplies?" The gambler's black eyebrows arched in question over steel blue eyes.

The captain scratched at a thick salt-and-pepper muttonchop sideburn that hid half of the left side of his face. He then tilted his head to the right, toward two smoked hams that dangled from hooks on the supply room wall. "You're looking at 'em. That's why I interrupted your poker game and brought you here. There ain't enough ham to feed the boiler deck passengers tonight, let alone handle the crew."

Chance frowned. Riverboat travel wasn't the luxurious journey along the nation's rivers as popularized in cheap fiction. The thundering pounding of the steam engines was deafening both day and night. Even aboard a lady as magnificent as the *Wild Card*, accommodations were small and cramped, with the majority of staterooms no larger than fifteen feet by ten feet.

However, the one thing the *Wild Card* offered was excellent cuisine, something often lacking aboard other paddlewheelers. Three times a day passengers were treated like royalty in the steamer's main cabin, feasting on meals prepared by the finest chefs on the river.

Nor did the *Wild Card*'s crew of roustabouts fight for sustenance from the "grub pile," scraps left over from passengers' meals, as was the case on every other boat on the river. Chance had eaten from the grub pile too often as a young boy when he had run away from his father's Kentucky farm to seek his fortune on the river. His crew ate hot meals three times a day.

"Suggestions?" The gambler turned from the two hams and stared at his friend.

"There's a new moon tonight, so we won't be running the river," Bert replied. "I'll pull into the bank and moor a couple of hours early. We can send men ashore to hunt for game."

Chance nodded; fresh meat would be welcomed by all aboard. "Count me among those going ashore. I could use the opportunity to stretch my legs."

* * *

Chance squatted beside a patch of moist dirt and pointed to the hoofprint at its center. "A deer—and a nice plump one from the deep cut of the track."

"I wouldn't argue with a venison steak to sink my teeth into." Tulley Young grinned while the gambler stood and cocked the six-shot Colt revolving rifle he carried.

The eighteen-year-old roustabout followed Chance's lead and thumbed back the hammer of the Sharp's breech loader in his hands. He then glanced over his shoulder. "How far you reckon we've come, Mr. Sharpe?"

"Chance," the gambler corrected while he tugged a wide-brimmed black hat securely atop a head of raven-black hair. "No more than five miles. We've only been gone two hours."

His gaze surveyed the Dakota Territory forest around them. Although most of the trees stood leaf-barren in the late autumn afternoon, he could not see the *Wild Card*—or even the Missouri River. His eyes lifted to the gray blanket of clouds that covered the sky. Enough daylight remained to track the deer for another half hour and return to the paddlewheeler before dark.

Chance smiled; a nice, fat buck would be a welcomed prize. Except for a covey of quail that took wing and flew beyond range before either Tulley or he shouldered their rifles, they had trekked through the unfamiliar Dakota forest without sighting a hint of game. Nor had the gambler heard any report of shots fired by the eight other hunters from the *Wild Card* who searched the wood for fresh meat. If the others' luck was as bad as Tulley's and his, the *Wild Card*'s passengers would go meatless tonight. The possibility didn't set well with the gambler. Venison steak and backstrap would assure the riverboat maintained its reputation for fine cuisine.

If not fine, at least adequate, Chance mentally corrected while he fastened the top buttons of the fleece-lined leather coat he wore. The late afternoon wind held the bite of coming winter in its teeth.

"I'll take the lead, if'n you don't mind, Mr. Sha—Chance?" Tulley glanced up the ridge on which they stood. "It's been a year since I last held a rifle. I'd like to get the chance at bringing down a big buck."

The gambler motioned the young roustabout higher along the ridge with a wave of his hand. "I don't care which of us gets the deer, just as long as one of us does."

Tulley grinned broadly with obvious delight and started up the incline. A smile touched the corners of Chance's mouth. Tulley's eagerness reminded him of himself when he and his father had hunted the Kentucky woods. This, however, was not Kentucky; it was the Dakota Territory.

Chance's eyes once more shifted over their surroundings. The gambler and young roustabout hunted rugged hills that strained upward toward the gray sky, trying to be mountains. No more than a thousand feet from base to crest, the hills were an incongruity of gently rolling mounds and abrupt jagged crests of bare, weathered rock. Sprinkled here and there amid the skeleton-stark leafless trees were an occasional pine, fur, or juniper, their green needle coats looking out of place among the late autumn grays and browns.

Four steps ahead of the gambler, Tulley held up a hand and halted. He knelt and pointed to another set of deer tracks that led to the right. Standing, the roustabout signaled Chance after him as he followed the deer's trail.

The forest thinned and opened before the two hunters when they circled to the western side of the hill. The trail they followed narrowed to a four-foot-wide ledge. Tulley knelt again, pointing to the tracks that led across the rock and dirt path.

"The deer came this way," he whispered when he stood.

Chance glanced to the right and a sheer drop two hundred feet below. A few hardy junipers clung tenaciously to ragged outcroppings of rock along the face of the cliff, but other than that there were no obstacles all the way to the talus-strewn forest floor below.

When the gambler's gaze returned to the ledge, he nodded for the roustabout to continue. With a four-foot width the path could easily accommodate a horse and rider; it offered no difficulty to two men on foot, even if they walked abreast.

"More'n one deer's been this way." Tulley tilted his head to the well-worn trail. "Looks like this is a regular path for deer in these parts."

"Right now, one deer will do quite ni—"

The rustle of underbrush at the opposite end of the twenty-foot ledge drew the gambler up short. The broad, shiny, evergreen leaves of a tight clump of cherry laurels shifted, a movement that was not caused by the constant wind.

Tulley's eyes gleamed with the light of a hunter who sensed the nearness of his prey. In a half crouch with the Sharp's held level at his waist, ready to be snatched to his shoulder in the blink of an eye, the roustabout edged silently along the ledge toward the dense wall of broad-leafed evergreens. Wary of the crunch of stone beneath the soles of his boot that might frighten away the animal they stalked, Chance cautiously moved after his young hunting companion.

A bestial roar echoed off the high-rising hills an instant before death tore its way through the fragile barrier of cherry laurels—death in the form of a thousand pounds of savage grizzly bear!

Standing three and a half feet at the shoulders, the brown-furred monster charged on all fours. Saliva streamed from yellowed fangs as its maw gaped wide and another thunderous roar tore from its massive chest and throat.

Tulley's rifle was halfway to shoulder when the grizzly struck. A black-clawed paw lashed out at the still-crouching roustabout. There was no time or space to avoid the beast's attack. With the full weight of its shaggy body behind the blow, the bear's paw landed solidly against the left side of the young man's neck. Crimson sprayed the air as claws rent vulnerably exposed flesh.

Yet, it was not those tearing claws that brought death; it was the sheer power of the blow. A horrible crack, the sound of Tulley's snapping neck, filled Chance's ears as he jerked the Colt revolving rifle to his shoulder.

As though its primitive instincts told it that the crumpling roustabout no longer presented a danger, the grizzly rose to its hind legs. With yellow fangs snapping, it charged.

Fighting past the panic that threatened to rob him of control, Chance took bead on the massive, furred chest, aiming for the beast's heart. His finger curled around the trigger and squeezed.

Nothing! The rifle's hammer clicked hollowly on a dud load within the chamber. The gambler's thumb arched up to recock the weapon, to advance the cylinder to the next round.

His thumb never touched metal!

In a speed that belied its bulk, the grizzly crossed the space separating Tulley's body and the gambler. Its left arm raked out, slamming into Chance's right side. Claws dug deep as they slashed through leather, fleece, and flesh.

A cry of surprised pain tore from the gambler's lips as the impact lifted him from the ground and hurled him into the rocky hillside. Unable to maintain his grip on the rifle, the Colt flew through the air and thudded to the ledge's dirt ten feet away.

Pushing the warm, sticky flow of blood that trickled down his side from his mind, Chance shook his head to clear the dazed blur from his eyes. Just in time to see the still-reared grizzly pivot and swipe out with its right paw again.

The gambler didn't think but acted. Shoving from the wall of rock at his back, he forced rubbery legs to dart to his right, away from the descending blow.

The gambit would have worked—had it not been for the snarling monster's unseen left paw. Tearing claws ripped into Chance's left shoulder, opening coat and flesh.

This time the gambler's feet managed to hold their contact with the ground as the hammering impact sent him reeling. Teetering at the brink of the sheer two-hundred-foot drop, he regained his balance and turned to face the roaring death that charged down on him once again.

With no escape to the rear, Chance took the only path open to him—he ran directly at the grizzly. His hope was that the beast would be so startled by the unexpected maneuver that it would retreat and give him the opportunity to dive for his fallen rifle.

That hope died at the end of a clawed paw that slammed directly into the center of his chest. Again the bear's strength lifted him from his feet and hurled him through the air. Only this time there was no hillside to halt his flight. There was nothing but empty air as the gambler was flung over the ledge.

TWO

A rush of adrenaline set Chance Sharpe's heart and temples apound like booming bass drums as he tumbled head over heels in a slow roll beyond the edge of the ledge. In the next instant there was calmness.

His past life did not flash before his eyes; regrets of things left undone did not flood his mind. Instead a sense of peace suffused his brain and mind—the peace of a man who accepts the inescapable inevitability of his own mortality.

That and an overwhelming awareness of everything around him, as though his senses sought to drink in the surrounding world in the few moments that remained before his body was shattered on the forest floor two hundred feet below. The acrid odor of his sweat and the warmth of the blood flowing from his open shoulder and side mingled with myriad forest smells. Every inch of his body was alive with the electric feel of his clothing against his skin, the force of the air as he plummeted downward. His ears heard the wind, the songs of birds, and frustrated growls of the grizzly above him. The gray of the overcast sky melted in the autumn browns and yellows before his eyes as he cartwheeled ever downward.

Nor did death come quick and clean. Time stretched about the falling gambler, seconds crawling by like minutes. Like a drunkard in alcoholic euphoria, Chance's brain numbed itself in preparation for that final instant of life. He transformed into a soaring eagle that rode the lofty currents of the air. He would fly forever!

The burning sting of juniper needles against his face snapped Chance back to reality. He crashed head first into one of the wind-twisted, stunted trees that had rooted itself into the rocky face of the hill. Refusing to admit the searing pain that lanced at his side and shoulder, the gambler threw open his arms; his hands went wide, grasping.

And found purchase!

Like vises, his fingers clamped about bushy limbs. Supple wood bent—bowed and sagged—and held! Violently Chance's body jerked around; his arms threatened to tear from their sockets. He slammed into the unyielding rock. A cry of pain wrenched from his lips. Yet he held! His hands refused to release the life-saving holds they had gained.

Risking a quick glance below, the gambler estimated he had fallen but twenty feet before snagging the scrubby juniper. Death still loomed beneath him. He had been given a reprieve; now it was up to him to make the best of it.

The panic he had avoided until now ate at his mind as his eyes searched the granite face of the cliff. Nothing! Except for a narrow crack in the rock in which the juniper had rooted itself, there was nothing. No hand holds, no eroded holes for his booted feet—nothing! Fate had given him this stay only to cruelly deny a pardon from his decreed sentence of death.

Nor was the reprieve to be more than mere seconds. Chance's fingers slipped. Grasping with every ounce of strength he could command from his hands, he clung desperately to the springy juniper limbs. The tree's needles, like a thousand pins, dug into his palms. Blood oozed from those small cuts, acting like lubricating oil. Inch by inch he slipped, unable to stop the inevitable.

It can't end this way! Chance's brain railed in the face of death. Releasing his right hand, he strained up to grasp a new, secure hold.

It was a mistake. The grizzly's claws had taken their full toll. His left arm and shoulder would not support his weight. Like a rope burning across his palm, the juniper's needles tore into his flesh as he slipped and once again plummeted toward the forest below.

Thirty feet he dropped, slamming back first into another of the stunted trees. Again his arms embraced the needled limbs; his bleeding hands clenched shaggy-barked branches. All to no avail—the roots of the precariously perched juniper ripped from the face of granite!

Head over heel, he tumbled again. He crashed into three more of the junipers, each snapping beneath his weight before he plunged into the top of a pine that pushed from the forest's floor. Like the junipers, the tree's upper branches popped and cracked to give way beneath their unexpected burden.

Chance's arms flailed; hands searched for purchase. He twisted and turned while he crashed through the long-needled pine, desperately seeking a branch strong enough to support his weight. His fingers found wood but lacked the strength to grip the rough-barked branches.

Pain exploded in his head. Red swirled before his eyes, pinwheeling into a flaring yellow that burst into searing white. Then the blackness of oblivion descended, and there was nothingness!

He heard the groan for long minutes before recognizing the sound as his own pitiful moaning. *Alive.* Realization penetrated the agony of his pounding head. *I'm alive.*

The gambler forced his eyelids to open. A rushing, swirling blurr of muted autumn colors spun out of control before his eyes. He blinked but could not steady the insane maelstrom. Lifting a hand, he tried to wipe at his eyes.

The movement was a mistake, he realized too late. His body, draped over a pine limb, slipped. Once more he fell. This time there were no branches to break his tumbling fall. Granite talus dug into his body when he struck the ground. Again pain erupted in his head, only to be swallowed by darkness for a second time.

Cold! He recognized the sensation that dragged him upward from the well of unconsciousness, through the throbbing agony that possessed his body. *Cold!*

Shivering, he tried to pull himself into a ball to fend off the biting cold. A cry writhed from his lips. Unbearable pain seared like a white-hot brand through every cell of his body. The cold could be endured, not the pain. He lay still, slipping back into the blackness.

His body burned. Where ice had dwelled now reigned fire. He remembered the cold and wished for its return. Above all he remembered the unrelenting pain that came from movement.

How many times had he awakened and foolishly tried to move? He had lost count, nor did it matter.

He caught that thought and held it. It did matter. He had to move—had to find . . .

Find what? It eluded him, concealing itself in the painfog that swirled inside his head. Something or someone was waiting for him, but he couldn't remember.

Have to find it. He grasped this thought and clutched it close. *Have to find it.*

In spite of the feverish flames that licked through his body he shivered. To find the evasive "it," meant that he had to move—must move!

But that also meant facing the agony.

No. Tears welled from his eyes in denial of what lay before him. *No, please, no!*

The undefined "it" would not be denied. It was life and death itself. He had to find it—if he were to live. He had to move, had to stand and find whatever waited for him.

So he forced himself to move. Beginning with the individual fingers of his hands, he twitched them one after another. Assured they were merely bruised rather than broken, he lifted his right then left hand. There was pain, but he could endure it.

His right arm moved. However, the fiery agony of his left had to be avoided at all cost. He then concentrated on his legs. Both ached and throbbed, yet he could detect no shattered bones.

Left arm, right side, head, he recognized the centers of pain in his body, pleased with what seemed a major accomplishment. *Protect them—and move.*

Gritting his teeth to fight back the bombardment of agony that screamed from the muscles of his body, he moved. Cautiously he sat up, waited endless minutes, then found the strength to stand on wobbly legs.

Now open your eyes, he ordered himself; time had come to walk out of the darkness.

He did; it didn't help. Blackness still enshrouded him!

Blind! Terror twisted inside his fever-burning brain. *I'm blind!*

Panic overrode the pain. Right arm groping the darkness surrounding him, he stumbled forward.

"No!" the single syllable came as a whimper from his lips. How cruel could fate be? How could he find the thing awaiting him if he could not see?

Chance's feet quickened their panicked shuffle. Blind or not, he had to find whatever it was that waited for him. He had to!

The ground slipped out from under his boots. Blinded he went down, flailing the air with his good arm. Somersaulting, he fell back into unconsciousness.

* * *

The darkness dissipated in the grayness of morning. Blindness had not robbed his eyes of light, he realized as he stared at the overcast sky, but merely night.

He slowly rose to his feet again and began to walk. The thing that waited for him was still out there, and he had to find it.

The demon crouched on its haunches atop a birch limb no thicker than a man's finger. In spite of the creature's massive size, that tiny limb neither sagged nor cracked beneath its bulk.

"Welcome to Hell, Chance." The demon's words hissed from tightly drawn lips of red mottled with glowing purple. "I've been sent as your guide."

"Guide?" The gambler leaned against the trunk of an autumn-barren aspen to support his fever-ridden body. "Hell? Am I dead?"

The horned-demoned laughed like thunder, his long, spiked green tail twitching. "Of course you're dead! No living creature is expected to endure agony such as that which gnaws at you."

"Hell," Chance repeated in disbelief.

"Come." The demon rose on the thin branch, stretching to its full height. Leathery brown wings crawling with lice spread from its back. "We've tarried here far too long. The Master summons you before him!"

Without warning the hellish creature launched itself into the air, hurling directly for the gambler with taloned hands outstretched to snare its prey.

"*No!*" Chance screamed. His right arm swung out, fist balled to smash into his tormenter's broad, flat nose.

Before knuckles contacted leathery flesh, the demon evaporated into thin air. One instant it was there, the next only the forest remained.

"Fever dream," Chance mumbled while he clutched himself and shivered. The fire that burned in his wounds was now devouring his mind, plaguing it with delirium.

Pushing from the aspen's trunk, he started forward again. There were no demons, he assured himself. *At least, not in this forest.* The horned creature was merely his mind playing tricks on him, trying to keep him from the thing that waited for him . . . out there somewhere. He couldn't let that happen—couldn't!

The howl of hounds echoed in the woods behind him. Twisting around, Chance stared in horror. Not "hounds" but one gargantuan dog charging from the trees. The baying voices that filled Chance's ears came from the creature's three heads!

Pivoting, the gambler ran.

Morning found him huddled beneath a mound of dried leaves he had scraped over his body to fight off the night's cold. Weak and shaking, he stood to peer at the flat gray of the clouds that blanketed the sky. He remembered three such mornings with their unbroken clouds, but he knew there had been more. Just how many escaped him.

As did his reason for being in this never-ending forest. Something had driven him through the featureless maze of trees, but he no longer could bring that into focus. Now only one thing brought his shuffling feet to motion, the primitive drive to slake the parched burning in his mouth and throat. Without water, he was a dead man—if he wasn't already.

He stood ankle deep in the icy water before his fever-clouded mind recognized the clear running stream. For a moment, he stood staring down at the crystal current that eddied around his scuffed boots. Then he sank to his hands and knees to lower his face to the cold water. Like some wild animal he slurped, drinking as fast as his lips and throat could work.

Gradually the burning in his throat subsided. With a grateful sigh, he lifted his head and sat back on his heels. The water was good and sweet tasting. He would rest, then drink again, sating the consuming thirst.

He blinked. Something moved beneath the water. There across the stream's rocky bottom it scampered. His right hand easied forward, fingers extended wide under the water. Inch by inch he moved closer until his open hand scooped down to enclose a crayfish.

Like a child with a pilfered sweet from his mother's cookie jar, the gambler clutched the crawdaddy to his chest while he stood and splashed his way to the stream's bank. There he settled atop a patch of moss and opened his clenched fist. The crayfish's antennae twitched, sensing open air. Its pinchers opened and closed.

Mudbug. The word thrust into Chance's mind. Someplace at sometime he had heard a crawdad referred to as a mudbug. Where? He couldn't remember. However, he was certain that he had eaten these vile-looking creatures before.

He was also sure that they had been cooked. A fire and pot were luxuries presently beyond his means. He did the only thing he could; he opened his mouth, stuck the crayfish's tail between his teeth and bit down.

Shell and meat alike he chewed and swallowed. The taste was bland, slightly fishy, and very gritty. It didn't matter. His stomach rumbled for a moment, then halted its protest as though recognizing the raw crawdad as food. In two more hasty bites, the gambler devoured the remainder of the crayfish—body, head, and claws!

Again his stomach rumbled; this time signaling the desire for more of the sustenance it had been denied. On hands and knees Chance crawled back to the stream's edge. His gaze searched the creek's rocky bottom. There in the shadow of a large rock he saw four black antennae!

Gently, so as not to disturb his intended prey, he eased a hand into the cold water. Carefully he positioned his open palm above the rock. Then in one flick of his wrist, he snared two more of the crawdads. Without hesitation, he wolfed down the first, then the second, and washed the gritty flavor from his mouth with another long drink from the stream.

Belly full and thirst slaked, he crawled atop a pile of leaves beneath a nearby tree, curled into a ball, and slept.

THREE

Chance awoke hungry and weak. Even with the burning fever eating at his brain, he recognized the relationship of those two conditions. His weakness, at least in part, stemmed from hunger. Except for the three crayfish, he had not eaten since . . .

The gambler blinked with uncertainty while he pushed to his feet from the bed of dried leaves. He couldn't recall his last meal before the crawdads. In truth, he couldn't remember where he was or how he had gotten here. The only blurred memories that floated within his fevered head were of the forest and his stumbling flight through the woods. As to where he fled—that too was lost.

Doesn't matter, he assured himself while he moved toward the gentle gurgle of the creek. That he knew where there was water and food was all he needed.

At the stream's edge, Chance lowered himself to his knees. He briefly drank to push back the dryness in his mouth left by the fever. When his head lifted, his eyes scanned beneath clear flowing water to the creek's bottom. Sidling between the protection of two large rocks, he saw the brown-gray form of a crawdaddy. His right arm stretched out, open hand positioned above the water. He hesitated but a moment to make certain the crayfish was unaware of his presence, then he plunged his hand into the icy current—and came up with his prey!

The creature's flipping tail went into his mouth, and he bit down, carefully chewing before swallowing. An instant of nausea swelled up from his stomach; he gagged but fought to keep the raw crawdad down. When the churning sensation in his abdomen subsided, he tore another bite from the crawdad and chewed, then popped the remainder of the creature into his mouth.

A wry smile touched the corners of the gambler's mouth. The moment of nausea surprised him. Had his first meal brought back more strength than he realized? It certainly had returned a portion of his taste. The flavor of raw crayfish lay heavy on his tongue, and another drink from the creek would not wash it away.

Like the whys and wherefores of his being in the forest, the crawdad's taste didn't matter. The crayfish was food, and food meant strength. He had to have more.

Again Chance's bleary blue eyes searched beneath the water's surface. His heart doubled its pace. Not a crawdad, but a fish now swam near the bank.

A fish—a real fish! His body trembled; saliva flooded his mouth. A single fish would surely equal half a dozen crawdads, if not more. He had to have that fish!

Pushing upward, he crouched on his haunches and waited. His temples pounded with anticipation as the fish darted closer to the bank. When it was within reach, his hand plunged into the water. His fingers closed around the slippery, scaly body—and held tight. With a flick of his wrist, he flipped the fish into the air and flung it back far onto the bank.

Turning, he watched the fish flip and flop on the dry land. Desperately it struggled to return itself to the life-giving water. He couldn't let that happen. Pulling a smooth rock from the creek's bottom he hastened to the fish. One solid blow with the stone and the fish no longer struggled.

Cross-legged on the ground, the gambler ripped into his meal with his bare fingers and began stuffing the raw flesh into his mouth. When only bones remained, he crawled back to the leaves and slept.

The light of another cloud-gray morning brought Chance from his sleep. As with the last time he had climbed from the bed of leaves, his stomach growled out its demand for food. The gambler returned to the stream to sate his belly's needs.

This time he sought fish not crawdads and found them swimming at the center of the stream. Without a thought to the water's chill, he shuffled into the creek, took a wide-legged stance, stuck his right hand beneath the water, and waited.

Minutes later, he was rewarded when one of the stream's finned denizens leisurely swam beneath his spread legs. The gambler's hand gently moved beneath the fish's belly, then jerked up. The fish came from the water in an icy spray of stinging droplets and landed far upon the bank, flopping and twisting.

Certain his meal could not work its way back to the creek, Chance once more took his position. Three fish moved between his legs before he once more succeeded in flinging one of the scaled morsels onto the bank. He didn't try for a third but scrambled from the water and dined.

His stomach had long since ceased to growl when he licked the last of the pink, raw meat from the second fish's skeleton. Wiping his mouth on an arm of his grimy leather coat, he rose and walked back to the stream for a drink. Although he could say nothing good about the taste of his fare, he had no complaints about its effects. With each meal he felt strength returning to his body, sensed the fever's fires gradually receding.

He lifted his right hand and gingerly rubbed at his left shoulder. Even beneath the crust of dried blood, he could feel heat radiating from the wound like a blazing furnace. The same fire burned in his torn side. Somewhere within his fever-ridden brain was the thought that he must drench these flames within his flesh.

Water kills fire, he thought while he drank.

After sating his thirst, he sat beside the creek and carefully removed his coat and shirt. Scooping handfuls of water from the creek, he bathed his side and then the shoulder. The water felt good, but its coolness wouldn't remain on his wounds. It trickled down his chest, back, and sides in icy rivulets that set his teeth to chattering—and the fire returned to the wounds.

His eyes containing a silent plea for help, he searched the forest and stream. His answer came from a broad patch of bright green that grew beside the water fifty feet upstream—moss!

Shirt and coat in hand, the gambler stood and walked to green. His fingers dug into the thick carpet of moss and tore out a wide, square-shaped swatch. He dipped this into the stream and gently lay it across his left shoulder. A smile uplifted his lips; the water's soothing coolness remained now.

Tearing out another patch of moss, he repeated the process on his side, then managed to tug shirt and coat back on. His left hand was just mobile enough to hold the second patch of moss to his side when he knelt for another drink.

"You're doing better, Chance," he spoke aloud to himself when he sat back on his calves and stared out across the stream. His head cocked to one side, and he repeated, "Chance."

For a long, silent moment he sat there, then said again, "Chance—Chance Sharpe." Uncertain whether he had forgotten it or not, he *was* sure that "Chance Sharpe" was his name. The feel of it was good on his tongue, "Chance Sharpe. Chance Sharpe. Chance Sharpe."

He leaned forward and stared at the image of a man—Chance Sharpe—reflected in the gently rippling surface of the stream. A rough coal pile of a beard, as black as the unruly, tangled mat of hair atop his head, covered his cheeks, chin, and the majority of his neck. In the reflection, he watched the fingers of his right hand lift and tentatively stroke his jaw line.

A week's growth, the thought pushed into his head. *Maybe longer since I knew the sharp edge of a razor.*

A week—maybe longer, echoed in his mind. Gradually the fuzzy swirl of his mind focused. He had been in the woods for at least a week!

Maybe longer. His fingers continued to idly probe the prickly growth of facial hair. Why was that important? Why should he care how long he had been in the forest? After all, he now had water and food. What else could he need?

The *Wild Card!* He needed to get back to the *Wild Card.*

"No!" The kneeling gambler shuddered. His eyes clenched closed as it all flooded into his head. He remembered everything, every brutal detail! He and Tulley Young had been hunting when a grizzly had attacked. Another shudder worked through his body when a vivid image of the roustabout's death filled his mind's eye.

The bear then attacked me! He drew a deep breath, accepting the memories of his fall over the cliff. Had it not been for the junipers and pine breaking his fall, he would now be dead. *Not that I'm much more than that now.*

But he *was* still alive. It was that thought that had driven him to search for the elusive "it." He now knew that real object of his search—the *Wild Card.* Even battered and lost in the delirium of fever, he had stumbled wildly through the woods, trying to return to the safety of his riverboat.

And managed to lose myself in these damnable woods! His eyes opened, and his head lifted to stare at the trees surrounding him. Like it or not, the truth was—he *was* lost. He had absolutely no idea where he was.

Bert Rooker will search for me. All I have to do . . .

He shook his head. There was nothing to be gained in lying to himself. He knew that his friend had certainly sent out search parties when he and Tulley hadn't returned from the hunt. But that had been at least a week ago. If they had found Tulley's body, they would have assumed that the bear had also killed him.

Gone! Hot tears of frustration blurred the gambler's vision. There was no reason for the *Wild Card* to remain when her owner had been killed by a grizzly. Bert Rooker was no fool; he would have continued downriver after a fruitless search to find his friend's body.

Pushing from the ground, Chance surveyed the forest. How alien it appeared now that he knew exactly what he faced. He remembered the Colt rifle the bear had knocked from his grip. If only he had the rifle. If only he had *any* weapon!

My knife! He reached down and extracted a slim, double-bladed stiletto from a sheath sewn inside the top of his right boot. The walrus-ivory–handled knife wasn't the Colt, but it was better than his bare hands.

Again he scanned the woods. There was nothing to be gained by remaining here. He had to make it back to the river. He recalled estimating that he and Tulley had only traveled five miles from the Missouri shortly before the grizzly's attack.

Five miles that might have stretched into fifty! There was no way to estimate the ground he had covered during his delirious flight. A man, even one ridden with fever, could travel a lot of ground in a week—or longer.

Chance's eyes returned to the stream. Armed with only a stiletto he couldn't expect to survive long separated from his source of food and water. The creek was the only avenue open to him. Like it or not, he had to follow it. Eventually the water's current would lead him to the Missouri, and the river would bring him to a settlement.

Stiletto clenched in his right hand, the gambler turned and started southward, following the stream's flow.

* * *

Two buzzards soared overhead. With their great wings spread wide, they silently rode the wind's currents in lazy circles. Chance watched their ever-revolving flight as he tread his way beside the still clear-running stream.

Were I gifted with wings, he thought, *I'd use them for more than flying around in circles.*

He lowered his gaze and mentally reprimanded himself for the idle thought. He didn't have wings, and there was little chance of a miracle that would suddenly bring them sprouting from his back. The task before him was enough; he had to make it back to the river. Wandering fantasies did nothing to hasten his feet or bring him closer to his destination.

Better to think about food, he told himself, or where his next meal was to come from.

His blue-gray eyes, containing a glint of light that had been gone from them for far too long, shifted to the forest that skirted the banks of the shallow creek. As he had for two days, since beginning the laborious trek downstream, he searched the tangled underbrush for any berries still clinging to leafless branches and stalks. He found none. Had they been there in the first place, birds migrating southward before the approaching winter would have stripped them long ago.

The gambler's gaze returned, as it always did, to the stream. Fish and crawdads would be the only items on the menu tonight. His face wrinkled in disdain. As strength-giving as they were, he longed for something—anything—to break the monotony of their taste. Even a crust of hard, stale bread would be like a king's banquet.

Chance shook his head. *I shouldn't complain.* His right hand lifted to rebalance the swatch of moist, cool moss riding on his left shoulder. His diet of raw crawdaddys, fish, and water were slowly bringing the desired results.

The fever that had licked at his mind and body for seemingly endless days and nights was no longer a constant furnace. Although it never broke, its flames were gradually receding, and his thoughts grew more lucid. Likewise, the damp moss he kept on his shoulder and side was working a magic of its own. The deep rents left by the grizzly's claws had closed and were slowly healing. Movement was returning to his left arm. While it was far from being fully mobile, he could use it to scoop dried leaves together for his nightly bed and to clasp the fish he ate.

If I only had a weapon. He glanced at the thin stiletto clutched in his right hand. *A* real *weapon!*

As deadly as the thin blade might be in a fight with another man, the slender length of steel had proved all but useless during the past two days. He had tried to hack his way through a sapling with the knife and found the task impossible. Lacking weight behind its edges, the stiletto barely nicked the wood even after a half hour. The knife simply wasn't designed to take the place of an ax.

Nor was it much use for throwing—or at least he didn't have the strength and eye to hurl the blade. He grimaced, remembering the rabbit he had seen come out of the woods to drink at the stream. Unaccustomed to man, the creature had almost walked right up to him. Chance had recognized that he was too weak to pounce on the animal, so he had cast the stiletto. Three feet from its target it had clanged off a rock. The rabbit, frightened by the sound, had scampered back into the forest.

In truth, the only use he had found for the delicate blade was skinning and gutting fish. The knife's razored edge was perfectly suited to that task.

Little more than a dining knife. Chance shook his head and let his eyes momentarily return to the sky. The two vultures had been joined by a third. The gambler's brow furrowed. Had the winged scavengers found a meal of their own? If so, it was close. The three birds practically circled overhead.

Chance found the answer to his question around a sharp turn in the stream. The creek's steep, muddy banks abruptly gentled on both sides to wide sand beds. There on the opposite side of the water lay a saddled horse!

Confused and uncertain, the gambler stood dumfounded. The deep, wild tracks in the sand and the animal's unmoving sides told the story. The ground had been too soft for the horse's weight. It had fallen and broken its right foreleg. A dark stain in the dirt about the animal's head spoke of blood flowing from a single shot of mercy to its head that brought a clean death and a quick end to its misery.

As Chance crossed the stream he saw other tracks in the deep, wet sand. These were human; the horse's rider had abandoned the dead mount and moved southward, following the creek's course just as he did. But what kind of man would leave his tack on a dead horse? A saddle and bridle were expensive items to leave behind.

Unless the rider knew there was help nearby! Hope sprung in Chance's mind. *He left the saddle and bridle, knowing he could come back for it quickly!*

A shift in the light breeze shattered visions of men riding in to rescue him. The unmistakable stench of rotting flesh hung on the breeze. The horse had been dead for three to four days! Its rider had left saddle and bridle behind because he didn't know how far it was to the next island of civilization in this rugged wilderness and didn't want to be weighted down by such a burden.

Chance started to turn and retreat across the creek to escape the putrid odor that rose from the animal—when his gaze fell on the saddlebags still lashed behind the saddle. *Food!* He ignored the overwhelming smell and hastened through the ankle-deep, sucking sand, driven by visions of a forgotten cache of jerky still tucked within the leather pouches.

He reached the dead horse's side and dropped to his knees. His trembling right hand tugged open the drawstring to the exposed bag that lay atop the animal's left haunch. Flipping the leather flap back, he dug inside—and came up with a single wooden box of matches!

"Damn!" He cursed aloud as he started to fling the box away. He stopped himself. Although not food, the matches would prove useful. The air grew colder day by day; a fire at night could be the difference between life and freezing to death.

Stuffing the box into a coat pocket, he turned his attention to the saddlebag wedged beneath the horse. Fingers still atremble in anticipation of some forgotten morsels within, he unlaced the tie strings holding them to the back of the saddle, then took a firm grip on the exposed bag and pulled.

Gradually, with the gambler wrestling the leather from side to side, the hidden bag eased from beneath the dead weight trapping it. Once again Chance dropped to his knees in the wet sand. He tore open the freed bag—and found a buckhorn-handled hunting knife within.

Refusing to accept the lack of food, his hand probed into each bag time and time again, until a scream of frustration pushed from his throat and rose to the air. Then he knelt there, head hung low and stomach growling.

Eventually Chance rose and began walking southward once more. Again the fates played with him. They led him to a feast of horseflesh only to reveal the banquet was tainted, fit only for the buzzards that circled above. They taunted him with saddlebags and hopes of crumbs left behind only to give him a box of matches and a hunting knife. If he survived these woods, it would be on his own and not with the help of the fates!

Chance easily hacked away the sapling's five branches and sharpened the young tree's tapered end to a point with the wide-bladed hunting knife. A smile uplifted the corners of his mouth when he hefted the makeshift spear.

He cursed the fates' cruelty too soon. The frustration of not finding food in those saddlebags had blinded him to the wealth he had discovered. He wiped the buckhorn-handled knife on his pants leg and tucked it securely beneath his belt. The blade had the length, width, and weight of a legended Bowie knife. Although not the ax he had wished for earlier, the blade had handily hacked through the sapling.

His smile grew while he strode to the stream. It had been years since he had seen such a knife. Before the war, hunting knives like this one were common atop every poker table aboard a riverboat. The dealer kept the knife there in plain sight. When a man lost the deal or didn't wish to handle the cards, he passed the buckhorn-handled blade onto the next player, an action that became known as "passing the buck." The term had quickly become part of the language, although its meaning had radically changed and now signified that a man shirked responsibility and passed it on to another.

A good omen. Chance patted the blade as he waded to the center of the stream. *A lost gambler's knife for a lost gambler. Maybe the fates* are *trying to tell me something!*

When he reached the middle of the current, he stopped and raised the sapling spear high into the air. A flash of silver beneath the water caught his eye. He tensed, watching a brook trout lazily swim in his direction. With only three feet separating them, the gambler struck. The spear shafted down, slicing into the water and skewering firmly into the fish's broad side.

Grinning from ear to ear, Chance lifted the impaled trout into the air. Things had begun to improve!

The snowflake alighted on the end of his nose, bringing his head up in surprise. The air was filled with the falling white.

"Son of a bitch!" He retreated from the water and quickly impaled the six fish piled atop the bank on his spear. How long had it been snowing? He had been so lost in the new found power of his spear that he hadn't even noticed the flakes. Now he had to find shelter—and find it fast.

A lean-to. The idea pushed into his head and was quickly discarded. Having the strength to hack through a single sapling was one thing; hewing down enough saplings to construct a lean-to was totally different.

Chance surveyed the forest on each side of the creek. No pines or heavy-coated junipers rose nearby. His gaze moved downstream. The creek's bed deepened as it cut through two of the high hills a half mile from his position. Of more interest were the granite boulders that lay strewn near the bank. If he could find two of the boulders close enough together, he could gather dead limbs and weave a makeshift roof between them. The shelter wouldn't do much to stop the cold, but it would keep the snow away.

Hastening as quickly as his weakened legs would carry him, Chance moved toward the boulders. He reached the first and immediately forgot his original plan. A hundred feet up the slope of the hill open a dark mouth—a cave!

The gambler scrambled upward and paused beside the entrance to sniff the air. No animal scent came from within. Cautiously he stepped inside.

The cave was small, extending no more than ten feet from its mouth to its rear wall. Tree roots dangled from the ceiling like a tangled mat of spiderwebs. However, it was dry and uninhabited; that was all he needed. Tossing down fish and spear, Chance worked back down the slope and moved to the woods. Tonight he would eat his first cooked meal in almost two weeks!

Chance tossed a dried branch as long and as thick as his forearm atop the fire. Cross-legged on a bed of leaves, he watched the yellow and red flames lick along the wood until it started burning. He then lifted a stick laden with a skinned brook trout from above the fire and began to eat.

He smiled; this was the last of his six fish and it tasted every bit as good as the first. A hot meal and the toasty feel of the small camp fire had completely reversed his outlook on his predicament. For the first time since realizing the truth of his situation, he felt as if he could survive.

In his coat pocket was a box containing thirty more matches. If he ate raw fish in the morning and built a fire only at night, that gave him thirty days to find a farm or a settlement. A month was certainly enough time to reach the aid of another human.

His gaze lifted to the mouth of the cave. Light from the fire danced off snowflakes that fell through the night's darkness outside. As big and as wet as they were, the flakes didn't stick but melted the instant they touched the ground.

I'm lucky this time, Chance thought with the realization that it wouldn't be long before another snow came and the temperature dipped below freezing.

His mind drifted back to the dead horse he had left a half mile upstream. His mind hadn't been clear when he had discovered the animal. Now he realized that he had left a wealth of raw materials laying on the sand. Tomorrow he would go back and collect all that he had overlooked.

In spite of the horse's stench, its hide could be easily cut into a cape to fit over his torn coat. His nose would accustom itself to the stink within a day or so, and there was no one else around to complain about the smell. There also might be enough hide left over to fashion some type of gloves or mittens to protect his hands from the cold.

Chance smiled while he popped another bite of warm fish into his mouth. One of these fish bones and a few strands of hair from the horse's tail would form a needle and thread with which he could mend the rents in his coat.

He could also use the saddlebags. Armed with his spear he could fish as he walked beside the stream. Each skewered prize would go into one of the bags until he was ready to eat.

I can use the bridle's reins, too, he thought as he considered a way to improve on his spear. If he split the narrow end of the sapling, he could wedge the stiletto's handle between the wood then bind it tightly with a piece of the leather reins. While virtually useless as a knife, the stiletto's twin-edged blade would serve nicely as a spearhead.

As he picked the last of the roasted trout from the bones, Chance eased the thoughts from his mind. Tomorrow would be soon enough to think about all the uses he had for the dead horse. Right now, he needed rest.

Stretching atop the bed of leaves, the gambler closed his eyes and drifted into a well-deserved sleep, undisturbed by the snow and cold beyond the shelter of the cave.

FOUR

The unyielding toe of a boot slammed into Chance's left side to painfully shatter dreams of dark-eyed delta queens elegantly strolling through moon-kissed gardens. The gambler groaned and clutched his throbbing ribs, and groaned again. The abrupt movement awoke a lance of pain in his still healing left shoulder.

"Get up, you murderin' son of a bitch!" a man's voice rudely demanded through the sleep cotton clogging Chance's brain.

Forcing his leadened eyelids open, the gambler stared at the blurry shape of a man hovering over him. He blinked to clear the sleep from his eyes. The man remained.

Chance groaned and rolled to his back. The delirium of his fever returned, haunting him with visions of other humans in a barren forest. Best to sink back into the comfort of sleep than to face the nightmares of fever dreams.

Again the boot jammed sharply into his side; the throbbing of his bruised ribs doubled. This time he only used his right hand to clutch at his side.

"I said get to your feet, you low life piece of dirt!" The vision's words came in a bestial growl. "Get up, unless you want to die right where you are."

For a second time, Chance stared up. The man who loomed over him was no fever dream, although the picture he presented was a nightmare. Cloaked in a shaggy buffalo-robe coat, the intruder looked more bear than man. However, the gambler's attention centered on the rifle the man aimed directly between his eyes.

"Get up right now or I'll empty this into your head." The man's right foot lashed out for a third time, slamming into Chance's side just below his clutching hand.

"Who—" Chance's words ended in a groan when the man's boot slammed into his side once again.

"You hard of hearin' or somethin'?" The intruder pressed the rifle's muzzle against the gambler's temple. "I told you to get on your feet. I mean *now!*"

Chance pushed to his knees then stood. His eyes met two dark, hate-filled orbs that glared at him from a face whose features were half-hidden by several days of bristly, unshaven beard. "Who are you? Why the rifle?"

"Ain't you the innocent one?" A humorless chuckle sounded like gravel as it pushed from the stranger's throat. "Who am I? Why am I holding a rifle on you? That's mighty nice. It might fool some of the others, but it don't work with me."

The man jammed the rifle into Chance's stomach. The gambler doubled over under the force of the impact and moaned.

"What did you expect me to do when I found you, you murdering bastard—greet you with a Fourth of July parade?" Pressing the end of the rifle's barrel under the gambler's chin, the man lifted Chance's head. He leaned close, his breath washing hot and sour over the gambler's face. "I'm just glad it was me that found you. Now I can take care of you the same way you gunned down my brother Wesley. The others want to make it easy on you. A rope's good enough for them—but not for me. Get on outside."

The harsh reality of his situation shoved away the remaining traces of sleep that muddled Chance's brain. For days he had silently prayed for a human rescuer. Now that one appeared, the man wanted to kill him! The gambler needed time to think, time to find out exactly what was happening to him.

"You've made a mistake." Chance's right hand eased toward his hip and the hunting knife tucked into his belt beneath his coat. The blade wasn't a fair match for the rifle, but at least it would give him a fighting chance. "I don't know you or your brother. I was attacked by a grizzly almost two weeks ago. I've been lost ever since."

Another mirthless chuckle pushed from the depths of the stranger's throat. His dark eyes narrowed. "Nice story, but you're forgettin' your horse. I found it dead about a half mile upstream. There ain't no way I'd mistake that gelding for another horse, not with the bar shoe it's wearing on its right forehoof. I been tracking that shoe for five days now, and I know it like I know the back of my own hand. Weren't nothin' to follow your trail to this cave. You been sloppy ever since you high-tailed it out of Beltin. Guess you didn't reckon on us chasing you this far east. But Frank Clancy don't let no man get away with shootin' down his brother."

"I didn't reckon on anyone chasing me at all. I never been to any place called Beltin. And, like I said before, I've never seen you or your brother," Chance answered. All the while he spoke, his fingers crept beneath his coat, working toward the buckhorn-handled knife.

"Oh, you saw Wesley all right. He's the bank teller you murdered back in Beltin, though I doubt you bothered to ask his name before you put two slugs of lead in his belly." Spittle flew from Frank Clancy's lips as he spoke, showering the gambler's face. "All that was on your mind was cleaning out the bank."

Clancy suddenly paused, and his dark eyes darted around the small cave. "Where the hell did you hide the money anyway?"

"There is no money," Chance persisted. "There's no money, because I didn't rob a bank. I told you that I've been lost in these woods for almost two weeks. I stumbled on that horse back upstream yesterday . . .''

Chance's words trailed off. His fingertips reached his belt—only there was no hunting knife nestled beneath it!

"This what you're lookin' so white about?'' Clancy held up the blade with his left hand while keeping the rifle trained on the gambler's midriff with his right. "Took this off you while you were sleepin'. Lose your gun when your horse took that spill upstream?''

Chance's hope sank while he watched Clancy toss the knife to the back of the cave. "My gun was a Colt revolving rifle—and I lost it when the grizzly attacked me. I found that knife yesterday in the horse's saddlebags. Before that, all I had was my bare hands.''

The gambler carefully avoided mentioning the stiletto sheathed inside the top of his right boot. Although never designed for survival in the wilds, the slender blade was quite capable of dispatching a man—if he could get at it!

"Now I know you're lying!'' Clancy laughed and shook his head. "Ain't no man able to live in this country with only his bare hands. Now get outside.''

When Clancy jabbed him with the rifle's muzzle again, Chance offered no protest. Facing the buffalo-robed man, the gambler edged toward the cave's entrance. He had to get at the blade in his boot without being too obvious. If he faked a stumble and fell as though he had sprained an ankle . . .

"Look, I don't exactly know who the hell you think I am, but my name's Chance Sharpe.'' The gambler's gaze darted over the cave's floor, searching for an object over which to stage his tumble to the ground. "I own the riverboat the *Wild Card.* I was hunting for—''

"I ain't interested in listenin' to your babblin's. All I care about is your dyin'.'' Clancy cut his words short. The man's eyes narrowed, hate and rage burning in their depths. "The others ain't here, so they ain't goin' to cheat me out of giving it to you the same way you gave it to Wesley. I'm going to gut shoot you and watch you die slow and hard."

"Listen," Chance tried again as he backed toward the mouth of the cave, "you're making a mistake. I'm not the man you want. I've never—"

The metallic click of the rifle's hammer silenced the gambler. Clancy's thumb edged back and his forefinger curled around the weapon's trigger. The rifle's muzzle dipped, homing on Chance's belly.

He's going to shoot me! Right now! The moment of truth had arrived. The instant Clancy's finger tightened about the trigger, Chance was going to die—slow and hard! Time for thinking had passed; only action would save him.

Chance's right hand shot out. In a short, chopping swing, he slapped the muzzle to the left, away from his stomach. Thunder exploded with the cave, its echoing roar rebounding off the walls and folding in on itself as the rifle discharged in a fiery flash of yellow and blue. The clouds of black smoke that always accompanied black powder billowed to fill the cave with an eye-stinging haze.

The thought of freeing the stiletto from his boot fled the gambler's mind. Through the smoke, he saw Clancy toss aside the spent single-shot rifle and go for a revolver holstered beneath the shaggy coat he wore. Smoke or not, at such close range Chance realized that he might as well be a sitting target for the man. He turned and took the only avenue that might save his life. He ran!

The morning's cold bit at his face and hands as he darted into the dull gray of an overcast sky. Here and there snow dusted the ground like a fine powder, testimony that the temperature had dropped below freezing last night. Drifts several inches deep piled about the bases of the boulders. It was between these sheltering boulder that Chance zigzagged while he bolted down the hillside toward the protection of the forest.

"You won't get away, you son of a bitch!" Clancy roared when he stumbled from the smoke-filled cave. "I'll get you, and I'll kill you just like you killed my brother!"

The harsh bark of a pistol sounded behind Chance. An instant later hot lead whined near his left ear as the shot ricocheted off a boulder to his right. Ducking, the gambler ran in a low crouch to disappear behind the thick bole of an oak.

"Sam, Jesse, I found the bastard!" Frank Clancy fired his six-shooter again, three shots straight up into the air.

The others! Chance's head jerked around. *He's signaling the others with him!*

"Bill, Ray, the son of a bitch is getting away!" Again Clancy pointed his pistol into the air and squeezed off the remaining two shots in its cylinder.

Chance didn't wait to watch the man reload. To the north he heard the hollow sound of approaching hooves—riders coming in answer to Clancy's shots. He had no intention of waiting around and greeting them. Shoving from the oak's trunk, he ran deeper into the woods.

An hour passed before Chance allowed himself the luxury of stopping and leaning his weight against a thin-trunked pine. He had pushed his weakened body beyond the limits of its endurance. His left shoulder throbbed, and his right side ached. Nor did his bruised left ribs let him forget the feel of Clancy's punishing boot.

Gasping to regain his breath, he surveyed the forest around him. He needed a hiding place and needed one fast. There was no hope in outrunning Frank Clancy and his companions. Even a man in perfect physical shape was no match for men on horses. Sooner or later they would overtake him. His only hope for escape lay in concealment—finding a hiding place where he could rest and regain his strength. He would wait out the day, moving only when night's shadows sheltered him.

A stand of five heavy boughed pines directly across a small clearing from his position caught his eye. *Take the high ground,* he thought wryly. Thick limbs able to support a man's weight grew high up on those ancient trunks, and the thick coat of green needles offered a dense cover to conceal him.

Chance glanced over a shoulder. His head cocked from side to side as he listened. No sound of approaching horses came from the forest. Equally important, he was unable to see any hint of a trail left by his flight. He had been damned careful to avoid snow patches and soft ground.

He turned back to the pines. All he had to do was cross the clearing and climb into those high limbs!

Forcing himself to move once more, the gambler carefully began picking his way across the open ground separating him from the trees. Each step he took shied away from the patchy snow that would give away his path.

"Hold it right there!"

Chance froze, ice flowing along his spine. From behind the very pines he hoped would shelter him rode a man astride a chestnut mare. A cocked Sharp's breechloader lay nestled firmly in the hollow of his right shoulder. Its muzzle was aimed directly at the gambler's chest.

Twisting, ready to bolt for the trees on his left, Chance halted before he took a stride. Another rider atop a dappled gray gelding reined from the forest. Like the first, he held a rifle cocked and raised. To the right a third man nudged a bay into the clearing. His thumb tugged back the hammer of the rifle he carried.

"Get your hands in the air," the first man ordered. His boot heels tapped his mount's flanks, edging the chestnut forward. A pleased grin spread across his unshaven face, revealing yellowed teeth streaked with brown tobacco stains. "Looks like me and the boys here figured right when we thought you'd run to the east. All we had to do was circle ahead and let you run right to us."

Chance lifted his right arm above his head. His left he held out straight before him. "I can't move the left more than this. A grizzly tore open my shoulder."

"That'll do. Just keep both your hands right where they are." The rider nodded to the man atop the bay. "Jesse, tie his hands behind him. We'll take him back to the stream and wait for Frank and Bill before we hang him."

All Chance's explanation of his plight bought him was a mouthful of knuckles. The three men had ridden with Frank Clancy to see a hanging and that's exactly what they were going to see. No matter that the man they intended to hang was innocent. Realizing that more words would add a broken nose to his now split lip, the gambler sat silently on the ground with his hands tied behind him and waited. Any thought of renewed flight was killed by the three rifle barrels that remained constantly leveled at him.

"Sam, what about the money from the bank?" This from the rider called Jesse. "We ain't seen hide nor hair of the money."

The man who had cut short Chance's escape into the pines rubbed a hand over his neck and shrugged. "It would make things a damned site easier if he'd spill where he hid the money, but it don't matter none. After we've stretched his neck, we'll find it. Couldn't have hidden it too far from where his horse broke its leg."

"Still wish we had the money." Jesse sucked at his teeth in disgust and glanced back to the gambler. "We could make your dyin' easier if'n you was to decide to tell where you stashed the money."

"I've tried to tell you that I don't know anything about a bank or any money," Chance started, then stopped. The disgust on Jesse's face was reflected on the faces of his two companions.

"He don't want to go out easy," said the rider the others called Ray. He shook his head. "Probably just as well. Frank's gonna want to watch him swing a long time after what he did to Wesley."

Ray leaned down in the saddle and jabbed Chance's ribs with the muzzle of his rifle. "Ever seen a man strung up at the end of a rope?"

The gambler didn't answer. Instead he tried to clear his head and focus his thoughts. There had to be a way out of this; he was just overlooking a possibility. The trouble was, that damned possibility remained hidden.

A cruel sound that vaguely resembled a laugh pushed from Ray's throat. "I was with Sherman down in Georgia. We caught us a Johnny Reb tryin' to steal some of our supplies. Hung him from a limb of an oak tree. Put the knot directly behind his head and not off the side. That way his neck didn't break. He must of jerked and kicked for an hour before he gave up the ghost."

"It ain't a pretty way to die, friend." Jesse stared at Chance. "Tell where you hid the money, and you'll go a lot easier than that."

"He'll find out just how hard dyin' is soon enough." Sam tilted his head toward the north. "Here come Frank and Bill."

The man turned to Jesse. "That oak looks stout enough to hold a man. Get him over there and get him ready."

Swinging from his mount, Jesse prodded the gambler to his feet and marched him beneath the oak. A few minutes later the remaining four men circled about.

"You want to do this, Frank?" Sam asked while he lifted a rope from his saddlehorn and tossed one end over a branch.

"I'll watch," answered the man who had entered the cave and awakened Chance. "Just make certain you do it right. I want it to take a long time for him to die. We owe Wesley that."

Sam nodded and spread a wide loop in the end of the rope he held. "Don't see no need to tie a hangman's knot. This will do the trick just as good. Jesse, tie off the rope around the trunk then get him up on your horse."

Chance's mind rushed as he stood helplessly and watched Jesse quickly knot the rope about the oak. Still, that overlooked something that would save his life refused to reveal itself.

"I better give him a hand. One man won't be able to get him in the saddle, if he starts to kickin'." This from Ray, who stepped from the saddle.

Both men roughly grasped the gambler's arms and hoisted him high. Belly down they threw him across the horse's back then jerked and twisted his body until he sat upright in the saddle. Sam nudged his mount to Chance's side, while Jesse kept a secure hold on his mount's bridle.

"Reckon it's proper to let you have your last words," Sam said. "If you got any, now's the time to spit 'em out."

Chance's gaze lifted, traveling over the faces of the five men who were fully intent on hanging him. Irony twisted the gambler's lips. He was only seconds away from death, and there was nothing he could think to say, not even a curse.

"You gave him a chance to say his piece." Frank's voice shattered the silence. "Hang the son of a bitch!"

Sam reached out, dropping the lariat loop over Chance's head. The rope bit into the gambler's neck as the man gave the makeshift noose one firm tug, tightening the knot directly behind Chance's head. Sam's right arm then lifted high, ready to drop down and smack the rump of the gambler's last mount.

FIVE

Senses numb and mind blank, Chance Sharpe sat astride the dappled gray and waited for the sharp pop of palm to horseflesh that would sound his death. He tried to think, but nothing would come—no plan for escape. The noose was set firmly around his neck, and there was nothing left to do—but die.

"Get on with it, Sam," Frank Clancy ordered. "It's time this gut-shootin' scum paid for what he done to Wesley."

Chance swallowed hard, struck by the realization that forcing a bit of saliva down his dry throat might be the last voluntary act of his life. Once the noose cut off his windpipe and death began to settle in, a man's kicking and twitching at the end of a rope was completely involuntary—muscles gone wild, struggling vainly to retain life.

"I'd freeze right there, Sam, just like you were covered in ice," a man's voice, one unknown to the gambler, called out. "Keep that arm high in the air, unless you have a hankerin' to die."

"John Tolbert!" The name hissed like a curse between Frank Clancy's drawn lips when the man's head jerked around, searching for the voice's owner.

Chance's own gaze followed the glares of his would-be murderers to a lone rider who nudged a broad-chested buckskin between two white-trunked birches. In spite of the youthfulness in the man's voice, the set of his square jaw and the determination reflected in his narrowed brown eyes spoke of a willingness to use the long-barreled Army Colt held in his right hand. The morning's gray light glinted dully from a tin star pinned to the chest of the green plaid wool coat he wore.

"Deputy, you ain't got no cause to go interfering with us." Frank Clancy's eyes narrowed to slits. His right hand tensed on his rifle, but the muzzle remained tilted toward the ground. "This is no concern of yours. We're just savin' the Territory the cost of a trial and a hangin'."

"Just doing your civic duty, huh, Frank?" There was no humor in the hint of a smile that touched the lawman's lips. His dark brown eyes shifted back to Sam. "I said keep that hand high, Sam Jardine. I don't want to shoot, but I will if you give me cause."

Sam's hand lifted higher into the air.

Chance swallowed again, his mouth feeling less cottony than a few seconds before. He didn't know this lawman anymore than he knew the five men intent on seeing him dance from the end of the rope around his neck. But it was more than obvious Frank Clancy and his companions did.

"Pull that trigger and you'll spook Jesse's gray." An oily slyness replaced the harsh bitterness in Frank's tone. "Sam's hand or the report of your Colt—either way this bastard will hang."

John Tolbert shrugged while the buckskin he rode moved closer to the men. "I've been following this man for five days, and I've got no want to lose him now. But . . . if I do, he won't be the only one to die. I figure that I've got time to get off at least three shots, maybe four—even five, before you can swing those rifles around. Be kind of hard to miss a target this close."

Chance felt tension radiate from his captors. Their eyes darted back and forth among one another and the deputy.

The harsh lines of their faces softened. None of them had the heart to try Tolbert's hand.

No one except Frank Clancy. The man's right started to ease up, intent on bringing his rifle into play.

A double metallic click sounded; Tolbert's thumb pulled back the hammer of the Army Colt. "Forget it, Frank. One Clancy's already died this week. Your ma and pa have only one son left. This man isn't worth dying for. He'll get what's coming to him after he's stood before a judge and jury."

Frank's rifle arm froze, but his face remained set with determination. Chance still could not breathe easily.

"He's right, Frank." This from Jesse who still stood with a steady grip on the gray's bridle. "None of us come along with you to get ourselves kilt. What difference does it make if'n we hang this whoreson or if the Territory does it?"

"Listen to Jesse, Frank," Ray spoke up. "All that matters is that the son of a bitch gets what's coming to him. Letting John have him just means we'll have to wait a mite more to see him swing."

Frank remained motionless, his eyes never leaving the lone deputy. The gambler could almost hear the gears grinding in the man's head. Was vengeance, even on the wrong man, worth the possibility of death? That was the choice Frank Clancy had to make. At the moment it looked like an even money bet to Chance that the man would go either way.

"Frank," Sam said. "Frank, we tried, but now—"

"You're wasting my time, Frank," Tolbert cut him off. "Make up your mind. If you want a shoot out, I'm willing to oblige. If not, get the hell out of the way and let me do my job. It's a long piece back to Beltin, and it's not getting any closer just sitting here."

Chance frowned with uncertainty. It was easy to see Tolbert's neck wasn't wearing a rope for a tie. If it had been, the gambler doubted that the deputy would have employed such a cavalier attitude.

"Back off, Frank," Sam urged. "We'll see this scum hang—one way or another. Me and the boys promised you that."

Frank's eyes turned to his companions, watching each of them nod. The tension flowed from the man's rifle arm, and his weapon dipped toward the ground.

"He's yours, John." Frank's head nodded warily. "Take him back to Beltin."

An overly held breath escaped Chance's lips in a long sigh of relief.

"Wise decision." An approving smile uplifted John Tolbert's mouth. However, the lawman's Colt remained raised and ready. "Sam, reach over nice and slow like and slip that rope from my prisoner's neck."

Prisoner? Chance didn't like the sound of that, but he wasn't going to argue. At least not right now. The best plan he could think of was to let the deputy do his job—for the time being.

"Slow and easy like." Sam's hand lowered, loosened the noose, and lifted the rope above the gambler's head. "Just like you ask, John."

Tolbert's Colt didn't move. "Now I want each of you to hand your rifles to Jesse there. And please don't any of you boys get any funny ideas. It would be a damned shame to have to kill one of you, especially since we're getting along so peaceful like."

One by one the four riders passed their rifles to their companion on the ground.

"Untie the rope from the trunk, Jesse," Tolbert ordered. "And bundle up the rifles nice and tight and hand them to me."

Jesse did as he was told. The deputy then tied the weapons behind his saddle, tugging on them twice to make sure they were secure. He then opened his left saddlebag.

When he looked up, he pointed the muzzle of his Colt at Frank. "One at a time each of you ride by and drop your pistols in this bag, starting with you, Frank."

For a moment Clancy hesitated before he threw open his buffalo robe coat and carefully lifted a six-shooter from the holster at his hip. He nudged his mount forward with a tap of his heels and deposited the handgun in the saddlebag. The four other men did likewise without a word of protest.

Chance watched, his respect for Tolbert's ability growing by the second. Not only had the lawman saved his neck, but the man had enough sense not to trust these five. Another less alert might have accepted their surrender and ended up in the dirt with a bullet in his back.

"Cut his hands free, Jesse," Tolbert directed the man on the ground with a tilt of his head.

Freeing a hunting knife, Jesse sliced through the rope binding the gambler's wrists behind him.

"Thank you. I was beginning to get a bit worried there for a moment." Chance grinned while he rubbed the circulation back into his hands and wrists.

"Don't be thanking me." Tolbert shot the gambler a scowling glance. "All I did was delay the inevitable. Folks in Beltin don't take kindly to having their bank robbed and one of their own shot down. You'll hang all right, but not today."

"Look, friend. I don't know who you think I am, but my name's Chance Sharpe. I own the riverboat the *Wild Card.* I was hunting for meat when a grizzly jumped me and one of my roustabouts. It's like I tried to tell these—"

"Save it for the judge and jury," the deputy cut him off. "Until then, I'd appreciate it if you'd keep your mouth shut."

Chance started to protest, then reconsidered. He sat silently.

"Boys, I hate to do this to you, but it's the only way I can make certain you don't try anything stupid before I can get this man back to town." Tolbert turned back to the five men. "I'm afraid that I'm going to have to take your horses."

"Our horses!" This from Sam.

"You ain't goin' to leave us afoot in this country?" Ray's jaw sagged in disbelief.

"That's exactly what I intend to do," Tolbert answered. "All of you climb down and hand your reins to Sharpe there."

Their pistols and rifles neatly packed away on the deputy's buckskin, there was nothing else they could do. Each man dismounted and handed his horse's reins to the gambler.

"You'll find your rifles and pistols about two miles upstream," Tolbert said while he reined his own mount behind Chance. "Would never think about leaving a man unarmed."

"But you don't mind putting us on foot!" Frank Clancy spat in disgust.

"Just for a day," the lawman replied. "I'll keep your horses with me until tomorrow morning, then I'll leave them tied by the stream. All except the gray, of course. Need the gray for my prisoner. That should slow you down enough to let me get back to Beltin a day before you. Hope you boys ain't got no hard feelings over this. It's the only way I can see to make sure I don't have to go and shoot someone."

Tolbert didn't give the five the opportunity to reply; he called out to the gambler, "Okay, Sharpe, move out. And don't try anything stupid or I'll finish what these men started."

The thought of that cocked Army Colt pointed at his back robbed Chance of a reply. He tapped the gray gelding's sides with his heels and started northward, leading four other mounts.

SIX

Whack!

The thudding sound of a knife blade biting into a pine trunk echoed along the creek. Immediately followed the ripping of splintering wood as John Tolbert twisted the steel to tear out a broad chunk of the tree. Fifty feet farther along the stream, the process began anew on the trunk of a birch.

Blazing a trail, Chance thought glumly. The deputy's purpose for hacking at the trees they passed was the only thing Tolbert had explained since they had left Frank Clancy and his companions afoot and weaponless.

"Unless you decide to come clean with it, I figure a couple boys and I will be riding back this way," the lawman had said. "Someone has to find that bank money. I'm blazing a trail to make certain I can get back to where you were found."

"And putting up road signs for Clancy and his friends," Chance had answered with no small amount of sarcasm in his tone.

Which was wasted on the deputy. Tolbert merely grunted. In fact, he merely grunted in reply to everything the gambler said whether it be a request for food or a few moments break to rest. Tolbert simply kept plodding northward, retracing the hard-traveled trail Chance had walked these past days. The only time he stopped was to drop the pistols and rifles to the ground as he had promised.

Chance had told him how stupid that action was, explaining that men on foot could easily overtake walking horses, if they were a mind to.

"And Frank Clancy is of a mind to," the gambler added. "You've just given him the guns he needs to overcome you and stick my neck in a noose!"

Tolbert grunted.

"You're not the most eloquent man that I've ever met," Chance conceded his losing battle to draw the lawman into conversation.

Or almost conceded. If John Tolbert wouldn't talk to him, then he'd damned well gab the deputy's ear off. He began to recount every detail of his misadventure, starting with the discovery of the tainted beef and pork in the *Wild Card*'s pantry. When he had finished, heard Tolbert's grunt, Chance began again with the same tale.

There was more than boredom behind the gambler's repeated telling of his run in with the grizzly. First he hoped that Tolbert would at least give his story half a listen. If not, he hoped that the constant chattering would lull the deputy and put him off guard. For Chance fully intended to escape. He still had the stiletto sheathed in his right boot. All he had to do was get at the blade and maneuver Tolbert close enough to employ the double-edged weapon. Colt or not, a man with a knife at his throat would damned well listen.

Chance's plan was simple; he had used it before quite successfully. Once Tolbert decided to camp for the night, he would fake a fall, grab his right ankle, and howl as though in deep pain. The instant the lawman approached to see what was the matter, the stiletto would jump free of its hidden sheath and press against Tolbert's neck. He would then disarm the deputy and ride to freedom. The gambler smiled as he remembered how easily he had taken a Texas sheriff with the same trick. All he had to do was wait until the right time.

Meanwhile, he started again, "My name is Chance Sharpe. I'm a gambler by profession and owner of a side-wheeler called the *Wild Card.* Nearly two weeks ago Captain Bert Rooker and I discovered that the *Wild Card*'s meat supplies had spoiled. The captain moored the riverboat early that evening, and I was part of a hunting party that went ashore in search of game."

"And you sighted the tracks of a deer," Tolbert cut in. "I know, Sharpe. I've been listening to the same story all day. You're wearing my patience mighty thin. Go through it one more time, and I'm liable to finish the job Frank and the boys started back there."

"You can talk!" Chance twisted around in the saddle and stared at the lawman. "I was beginning to think you had suddenly been struck dumb!"

"Deaf would be a greater blessing," Tolbert answered dryly. His dark brown eyes met the gambler's gaze without blinking. "Didn't your mama teach you that it was bad manners to go around squawking like a blue jay all day?"

"Not half as bad as hauling a man off to jail for a crime he didn't commit—or even know about," Chance replied. "Do you realize that I'm not certain why those men back there were so dead set on stretching my neck?"

Tolbert's eyes narrowed, and his mouth twisted in disgust. "You're either as stupid as they come, Sharpe, or you've got a damned good act."

"You miss on both counts," Chance said with a shake of his head. "There's a third possibility that you seem to keep ignoring—that I'm innocent and don't know what the hell is going on!"

The deputy's head lifted and he stared at the late afternoon sky. "It'll be getting dark soon. We'd best find us a spot to camp for the night."

"Dammit, man! Can't you get it through your head, I don't know why you're dragging me off to some godforsaken town called Beltin!" The gambler refused to let the matter drop. "At least have the decency to tell me what it is I'm supposed to have done!"

Tolbert's chest heaved, and he said, "Last Saturday Beltin's bank was robbed of ten thousand dollars, and the teller was killed. That teller was Wesley Clancy, Frank's younger brother."

"I can understand a man wanting to get his brother's killer," Chance said, "but that doesn't explain why Clancy picked me."

"A stranger rode into Beltin Saturday before the bank was robbed. Nobody could find hide nor hair of him after the robbery. Two plus two says the robber could be that stranger."

"It still doesn't add up to me," Chance verbally stood his ground. "Or does any stranger fill your bill?"

"This one was riding a horse with a bar shoe. Its tracks and that of another horse lead away from the bank." Tolbert's gaze surveyed the forest. "I followed the bar shoe east while Sheriff Pardee headed north after the other tracks. That horse lying dead back by the creek was wearing a bar shoe—the same one I've been following."

"But it wasn't my horse." Chance recounted how he had stumbled upon the dead animal.

The deputy's answer was another noncommittal grunt. He nodded to the right. "The ground looks soft over by those oaks. We'll camp there for the night."

Chance reined the gray toward the stand of five oaks, halting when Tolbert told him. He then dismounted under the lawman's watchful eyes and tied the gray and the other four horses he led to the tree's lower branches.

Now, Chance thought while he finished knotting the last of the reins. This moment was as good a time as any to fake his fall.

Stepping from under the trees, he started toward Tolbert. He took three steps when he purposely twisted his right foot, cried out, and fell to the ground. As to his carefully thought-out plan, he howled in mock pain and clutched at his right ankle. The action allowed him to raise the cuff of his pants and bring the stiletto within reach of his fingertips.

The plan worked perfectly, except for one vital element: Tolbert didn't rush to his aid! The deputy simply sat astride the buckskin and stared at the gambler. "You ought to be more careful where you step."

"I think it's broken." Chance clung to his role of the injured man.

"Doubt it." Tolbert shook his head. "I didn't hear anything snap. You usually can hear a bone when it goes. You probably just sprained it a mite. Rub it a little, then get up and walk around. It'll go stiff on you if you don't."

Chance stared at the lawman as he dismounted and tied the buckskin beside the other horses. *Damn!* The gambler glowered. The deputy was either smarter than he appeared or the stupidest man Chance had ever met. No matter which, his ploy wasn't working. All he could do now was maintain the role so that Tolbert wouldn't grow suspicious.

Acting as though taking the lawman's advice, Chance massaged his ankle, then carefully rose. Gingerly he placed his weight on the leg and limped around a bit under Tolbert's watchful eye.

"Guess you were right," he finally said to the deputy. "Looks like I just sprained it a little."

Tolbert nodded as he dug into a saddlebag. "Now strip off all your clothes."

"What?" Chance stared at the man, uncertain he had heard correctly.

"I didn't whisper. I said take off every stitch of those clothes." When Tolbert turned, he leveled the Colt at the gambler. "Strip."

Chance began to peel away the layers of his clothing, beginning with his torn coat. "I don't know what you have in mind, but—"

"What I have in mind is saving my nose from what it's had to go through all of today. I've been riding downwind of you, and it's been all I can do to keep from gagging." Tolbert tossed Chance a yellow bar of lye soap that he had pulled from the saddlebag with his left hand. "Take yourself over to that stream and bathe."

"I didn't realize that I had offended your delicate sensibilities." The gambler glared at the lawman, still unable to believe Tolbert was ordering him to bathe.

"It isn't my sensibilities that are offended. It's my nose. Sharpe, you stink. If a polecat got a whiff of you, he'd turn tail and run." The deputy used the Colt to point to the stream. "Bathe! You might even find that you take a shining to it."

"But that water's like ice!" Gooseflesh rippled over Chance's legs when he dropped his breeches and stood before the lawman. His teeth chattered as he spoke. "I'll freeze to death!"

"I doubt it." Tolbert's expression was that of a man unmoved. "While you bathe, I'll gather wood and get a fire going."

"Taking a risk leaving me alone while you're traipsing around in the woods, aren't you?" The gambler unbuttoned his shirt. "Aren't you afraid that I'll try to escape?"

"If you want to make a run for it, go right ahead." Tolbert shrugged. "A bare-assed naked man isn't going to get too far. I'm not going to worr . . ."

The deputy's words trailed off, and his eyes narrowed when Chance slipped off his shirt then removed the patches of moss covering his shoulder and side. The lawman moved directly before the gambler and examined the wounds.

"I don't know if a bear made those or not, but something definitely has been after you!" Tolbert shook his head. "Clean those up good. I've got some sulfur to sprinkle on them. Bound to be better than that moss."

"A bear did this, just as I've been trying to get into that thick skull of yours." Chance turned and walked into the icy, clean stream. "Damned difficult for a man to rob a bank when he's torn up like this."

"Could've happened after you robbed the bank," the lawman called after him. "Those scratches don't change a thing."

"Scratches!" Chance snorted in disgust as he walked to the middle of the stream, gathered his courage, then plopped hindside down in the current. He had only *thought* the water had been cold. Without the protection of his clothing, he now knew the creek was ice frigid. There was no way to stop the clattering of his teeth.

"Try rubbing that soap over you," Tolbert shouted from the bank. "That should warm you up some."

Chance did just that; it didn't help. However, it did remove the protective layer of dirt and grime his body had accumulated since he had been separated from the *Wild Card,* which only doubled the bone-chilling cold.

"While you're at it, you might try giving these clothes a washing."

The gambler's head snapped up, and his heart skipped a beat. Tolbert was gathering his clothing from the ground!

"My, my, look what we have here." The lawman lifted Chance's boots and extracted the walrus-ivory–handled stiletto from its sheath. "No wonder you went and hurt your ankle. Damned lucky you didn't cut your foot off carrying something like this around."

Tolbert's eyes lifted to the soaking-wet gambler, giving him the reprimanding look of a parent correcting a wayward child. "I wouldn't want that happening to anyone in my custody, so I'll just keep this little pig-sticker."

Dropping the gambler's clothing in a heap at the water's edge, Tolbert turned, deposited the stiletto in his saddlebag, and walked into the woods.

"Son of a bitch!" Chance's frustration refused to be contained. That blade had been his only hope of escape!

Tolbert slid one of the two spitted rabbits into a tin plate and passed it to Chance. "Serve yourself the beans."

The gambler ladled five heaping spoonfuls of the navy beans and bacon onto the plate. The deputy handed him a spoon that he wiped clean on the thigh of his trousers.

"Usually I let a prisoner use a knife to eat," Tolbert said with a wry smile at the corners of his mouth. "But I get the feeling a butter knife would be a dangerous weapon in your hands, Sharpe."

"Chance," the gambler corrected while he tore a leg from the roasted rabbit and sank his teeth into the savory meat.

"I'll stick with Sharpe." Tolbert filled his own plate with the remaining rabbit and a healthy helping of beans. "If I started calling you by your Christian name, you might get the idea that we were friends or something. And believe me, Sharpe, friends are the one thing we aren't."

Chance only half listened to the deputy's words. His mouth, tongue, and stomach were celebrating their reunion with food—*real food!* He had dined on fish and crawdads so long that he had almost forgotten what red meat was.

"Though I have to admit you're a mite easier to take now that you've had yourself a bath." Tolbert chuckled. "How's your shoulder and side feeling?"

Chance didn't pause in wolfing down three consecutive spoons laden with beans to answer. He merely nodded. Although he would never admit it to the lawman, the bath itself had felt good. His own nose had numbed itself to his stench; he could only guess at the full power of the stink he had carried.

"Your clothes are about dry. Sprinkle more of that sulfer on your wounds before you get dressed," the deputy ordered.

Chance tugged the blanket wrapped around him closer to his naked body. "Mind if I finish eating first? After gnawing on raw crawdads and fish, this tastes like it was prepared by the finest chefs in New Orleans."

"No one's stopping you. Have the rest of the beans, if you're a mind. I've got enough for me on my plate." Tolbert lifted two tin cups from the ground and filled them with coffee, which boiled in a pot set beside the camp fire.

Chance accepted one of the cups and drank, not even minding that the hot brew scalded his mouth and throat. "Damn that's good! At one time I never thought I'd taste coffee again."

The deputy's dark brown eyes lifted to the gambler, and the amused smile at the corners of his mouth evaporated as his expression sobered. "You'd make things a lot easier on a lot of fine people, if you come clean."

Chance chuckled. "I am clean. That was me sitting out there in the stream, scrubbing with lye soap—remember?"

Tolbert's expression remained unchanged. "That ten thousand you took from the bank meant a lot to the people of Beltin. It represents the life savings of more than a few hard-working, God-fearing people. You cleaned us out, practically ruined the town."

The gambler's cool blue eyes peered at the lawman over the rim of the tin cup. John Tolbert wasn't a man to be underestimated. In spite of his age—Chance placed him at twenty-seven, give or take a year—the deputy had more than a few tricks up his sleeve that bespoke of a maturity and experience that couldn't be measured by mere passage of time. Only now did the gambler realize that the bath had been a ruse so that the lawman could search him for any hidden weapons—a ruse that had worked quite successfully. Atop that, Tolbert lulled him with a hot meal in the hope he would slip and reveal where the stolen money had been hidden. Yes, John Tolbert was quite a wily man, and he had probably tripped more than one criminal with his easygoing manner. Only this time he wasn't dealing with a criminal.

"I've told you a couple of hundred times today that I'm not the man you want, Tolbert." Despite the hunger still growling in his stomach, Chance set his plate and cup aside. "Your backwoodsey hospitality isn't going to change that."

The deputy grunted, obviously still unconvinced. "Have it your way, Sharpe. A jury isn't likely to believe your story anymore than I do."

The gambler stood and began to dress. "If that's the case—and if I *were* your bank robber—then I'd have nothing to gain by telling you where the money's stashed away, would I?"

Tolbert answered by standing and walking to the gray gelding. He untied the sleeping roll from behind the saddle and tossed it to the gambler. "If you're through eating, you'd best get some sleep. We'll be on the trail again before sunup."

Chance spread the blankets before the fire and climbed into them. He intended to be on the trail again hours before that—nor would he be traveling with the lawman.

Chance waited until John Tolbert's breathing shallowed to the soft, gentle rhythm of sleep, then he waited some more to assure himself that the deputy was indeed lost in dreams. Perhaps he had overestimated the lawman earlier. Tolbert hadn't bothered to tie or cuff his hands before the gambler had turned in for the night. That was a mistake the deputy would never forget!

Slipping an arm from beneath the sleeping roll, the gambler's right hand found a fist-sized rock, which he had sighted earlier, and pulled it to him. The rock wasn't his stiletto, but it would do the trick. Once he had his hands on Tolbert's rifle and pistol, he'd have nothing to worry about.

Chance edged back the blankets and pushed to a sitting position. His gaze traveled across the flickering flames of the low-burning camp fire. Tolbert slept unmoving, bundled in his own sleeping roll with his back to the fire. *So far so good.*

Cautious of unwanted noise, the gambler gradually rose to his feet. The deputy still lay motionless, unaware as Chance crept around the fire to crouch behind the man. Rock clenched tightly, the gambler's right fist rose above his head.

The double metallic click of a cocking revolver sounded in the night.

Chance's gaze dropped. The muzzle of Tolbert's Army Colt stared out at him from beneath the deputy's blankets!

"I was hoping that this wouldn't happen." Disgust washed over Tolbert's face as he rolled to the gambler. "It would have been a lot easier on both of us if you hadn't taken a mind to pull a stunt like this."

A rock was absolutely useless in the face of a cocked six-shooter. Chance tossed it aside and shrugged. "The possibility of being hanged for a crime that I didn't commit makes me do foolish things. Nothing personal, you understand."

"Hard not to take it personally. Having one's skull bashed in is about as personal as you can get." Tolbert stood; the Colt remained leveled at the gambler's chest.

"About as personal as having my neck stretched for robbing a bank and killing a man I never saw."

"Like I've been trying to tell you, whether you're guilty or innocent isn't up to me. That's the job of a judge and jury.'' Tolbert motioned the gambler toward a tall sapling near the oak where the horses were tied. ''My job is to bring you in.''

When they reached the tree, Tolbert pulled a pair of handcuffs from a back pocket and bound the gambler's arms around the base of the tree. ''That should hold you until I've had myself a nap.''

''You mean that you're going to leave me here all night? I can't sleep this way!'' Chance protested.

''Should have thought of that before you got them foolish ideas in your head.'' Tolbert tilted his hat at the gambler then returned to the warmth of the fire and his blankets. Within seconds he snored loudly, leaving no doubt as to whether he slept or not this time.

''Bastard!'' Chance cursed beneath his breath.

His gaze ran upward to the tree's twenty-foot top. He could never climb his way out of this; the branches over his head would never support his weight. Nor was he able to bend the trunk itself. It would take a team of oxen to break wood a foot in diameter!

Sinking to the ground, Chance cursed until he began to repeat himself. It didn't help; lost in sleep, Tolbert even robbed him of the pleasure of his biting insults. All Chance could do was shiver and wait for the morning.

SEVEN

The sign read:

BELTIN
Population 1101

Beside the tally someone had scrawled in black paint: ½.

Chance nodded to the sign and lifted his eyebrows in question when he looked at Tolbert.

"Our mayor's got a strange sense of humor. He came back from the war minus a leg and an arm," the deputy explained with a shrug. "After he was elected last November, he took a can of paint and a brush and painted that in. Don't let the one half fool you. Charlie Bowden remains all man, in spite of a missing arm and leg."

"Strange sense of humor" doesn't describe the mayor's action, Chance thought as Tolbert motioned him down a road that led to the small town. *"Morbid" is closer to it!*

As deputy and prisoner rounded a gentle, sweeping curve in the wagon-worn trail, the final destination of their five-day ride came into view. The slight incline—it was far too minor to be dubbed a hill—placed the two riders above Beltin, giving Chance a clear view of the prairie hamlet. Whitewashed homes sprinkled the autumn-brown grasslands around the town's two central streets, whose intersection marked the heart of the community. More whitewash covered many of Beltin's buildings. Others showed flaked traces of red and yellow paint, while the remaining structures stood gray and weathered, never knowing the protection of a coat of paint.

Beltin's residents moved along the hamlet's only two avenues while Tolbert brought his prisoner through the center of town. Whether they walked, sat on horseback, or held a team under rein, man and woman alike stopped and gawked as the deputy lead his prisoner westward.

"Nothing like Dakota hospitality to make a man feel welcome," Chance grumbled as he returned the stares of Beltin's townsfolk. "You'd think that I had small pox by the looks on their faces."

"Worse," the lawman said. "You stole every penny most of these people had to their names. Can't blame them for wanting to get a good look at you."

"They're definitely not shy about getting an eyeful," the gambler answered without humor. "Some of them look like their eyeballs are about to fall out."

"You won't have to worry about their stares much longer. These cells have high windows." Tolbert drew his buckskin to a halt and tilted his head toward a single-story wooden building.

Chance stared at the bleak, unpainted structure set near the western edge of a street proclaimed to be MAIN by a white and black sign. A wooden shingle, hanging on two chains above the door, read JAIL. He didn't need the sign to tell him that they had finally arrived. All frontier jails looked the same.

"Inside," Tolbert ordered.

Hands still cuffed, the gambler grasped the saddlehorn and swung to the ground. He looped the gray's reins around a hitching rail, then waited for Tolbert to take his arm and push him toward the jail before entering the building. After all, there was no reason for making this any easier on the lawman than necessary. *He* was the wronged party—not the deputy.

"Someone there?" a man's voice called out from behind a door at the rear of the jail's single-room office when Tolbert closed the front door.

"Sheriff Pardee," the deputy answered. "It's me."

"John?" The office's rear door opened and a ruddy-faced, clean-shaven man with a slightly bulging belly stepped into the office. From the streaks of white in his brown hair, Chance estimated the newcomer to be in his fifties. The sheriff's beaming grin that greeted Tolbert transformed into a perplexed expression when the man's gaze shifted to the gambler. "Who's this, John?"

"The stranger riding the horse with the bar shoe," the deputy answered while he hung his hat on a wooden peg inset on the office's wall. "He calls himself Chance Sharpe. Took me five days to ride him down. Wasn't more than two miles from the Missouri when I caught up with him."

Chance's head jerked around, and he glared at the deputy in disbelief. He had been that close to the Missouri River? Now he was at least a hundred miles west of the Big Muddy in a town that wanted to see him hanged!

"Lucky I found him when I did," Tolbert continued to outline his chase to the sheriff. "Frank Clancy and four of his friends caught up with him first. They were about to lynch him when I rode in. Didn't have any trouble with Frank or the others. Afraid that if I had, I would have let them have him."

Grand! Chance thought, barely able to keep from voicing his exasperation. He had been closer to dancing from the end of a rope than he had realized.

"Damned lucky you were able to stop them," Sheriff Pardee replied with a worried shake of his head. "If you hadn't, we'd be hunting them down for murder right now."

"What?" Tolbert stared at his superior. "What are you talking about, Glen?"

Pardee nodded at the gambler. "The fact that this ain't the man we were after."

"Finally someone with a shred of sense about him," Chance said.

And was ignored.

Furrows of doubt deepened across Tolbert's forehead. "What do you mean this isn't the man?"

"I found our man about an hour out of town," the sheriff explained. "It was Martin Ranson who robbed the bank and killed Wesley Clancy."

"Martin Ranson?" Tolbert sank into a chair beside a potbelly stove. Doubt still wrinkled his brow when he repeated, "Martin Ranson?"

"Now that we know it wasn't me," Chance tried to interrupt, "would either of you gentlemen of the law care to remove these cuffs? I believe there's still laws concerning false arrests."

Neither sheriff nor deputy paid him heed. Pardee sucked at his teeth and nodded. "I found Martin Ranson north of town. He still had the bank's money bags in his saddlebags."

"The handcuffs, gentlemen." Chance held out his arms.

"What about the money?" Tolbert questioned. "Didn't he have it on him?"

The gambler's eyes rolled in frustration. "All this is extremely interesting. And I'm certain both of you want to discuss it at length. But let's be reasonable . . ."

"Only five dollars he had stuffed in a shirt pocket." The sheriff walked behind the office's sole desk and sat in a chair. "The bastard won't talk either. Says his pa will take care of things."

"He's not blowing smoke, Glen. Old man Ranson's not the kind of man to take kindly to having his youngest son behind bars—no matter what he's done,'' Tolbert said. ''Have you had any trouble out of him?''

''Been lucky so far. Clay and his other sons are up north in Longway. Don't expect them back for a day or two,'' Pardee replied. ''But when they get wind of Martin being locked up, I expect they'll see that we earn our pay this month.''

Tolbert shook his head. ''I don't look forward to tangling with any of them. Each of those boys has a mean streak a mile wide.''

''And their daddy's twice as ornery,'' the sheriff added. ''I might have been able to smooth things out if Martin hadn't gone and gunned down Wesley Clancy. But the town's not going to stand for murder, even if we can get the bank's money back.''

''The handcuffs!'' Chance insisted.

And still went unheard. Tolbert asked, ''What about a U.S. Marshal? We're just local officials. The feds will have to handle the trial.''

''I've wired for a marshal to come and take Martin to Fargo for trial.'' The sheriff nodded. ''Got an answer three days ago. No one will be making the circuit for at least another month. Until then, he's our problem.''

''Damn!'' Tolbert wiped a worried hand over his face. ''Things could get mighty sticky around here before that. Have you considered deputizing some of the men in town? If Clay Ranson and his boys decide to cause trouble, we'll need extra hands—and guns.''

''Speaking of hands!'' Chance stepped directly between the two lawmen and demanded, ''What about these hands!''

Pardee finally looked up at him as though he had totally forgotten that the gambler was present. ''Sorry, Mr. . . .''

''Sharpe, Chance Sharpe,'' the gambler said, making no attempt to disguise his irritation. ''I'm the one your deputy dragged here all the way from the Missouri River, remember?''

''Take the cuffs off him, John.'' The sheriff waved Tolbert to his feet and watched while the deputy unlocked the handcuffs. ''You're free to go now, Mr. Sharpe.''

Chance's jaw sagged. His head cocked from side to side as though he had missed what the sheriff had said. ''That's it? 'You're free to go'! Not even an 'I'm sorry for the inconvenience we've caused you'?''

''I don't think I'm getting your point, Mr. Sharpe?'' Pardee blinked at him.

''What I'm getting at is that your deputy just dragged me a hundred miles away from the Missouri River. I haven't got a horse or a gun. My clothes are tattered from a bear who took a disliking to me. I haven't got a penny in my pockets, and all you can say is 'you're free to go.' Just like that with no mind to the fact that you've stranded me here in the middle of nowhere!'' Outrage tinged each of the gambler's syllables.

Pardee leaned back in his chair, pursed his lips, and scratched at his neck while he studied the gambler. Eventually he shrugged. ''I still don't see that you've got a complaint, Mr. Sharpe. The way I reckon it, you'd be buzzard bait right now if it wasn't for John here. Frank Clancy was about to string you up, wasn't he?''

Chance blinked in surprise. Caught off guard by the lawman's twisted logic, words failed him. All he could do was sputter incoherently.

''Yep''—the sheriff nodded—''the way I figure it, you owe my deputy a thank you for saving your neck.''

The gambler found his tongue. ''I'm not complaining about being saved from a lynching. I *am* complaining about being falsely arrested and dragged halfway across the Dakota Territory to a town nobody but the people living here ever heard of, then you dismiss me as though I didn't exist. I'm a hundred miles from the Missouri River with slim prospects of getting back! I think it reasonable to believe you and your deputy will assume partial responsibility for my being in this condition."

"What'd'ya say was his trade, John?" Pardee glanced at Tolbert. When the deputy replied "gambler," the sheriff shook his head. "Would've fooled me. Long-winded like that, I'd have thought you were a lawyer, Mr. Sharpe." Pardee paused to scratch at his neck again. "But I reckon you do have a legitimate concern. The town of Beltin will see that you have transportation back to the Big Muddy on the first wagon heading east."

Chance smiled; now he was getting somewhere! "When will that be?"

"Next week," the sheriff replied, "or maybe three months from now. Depends. Winter's starting to set in. Not many people travel east come winter in this part of the country."

"Months!" The gambler was flabbergasted by the lawman's casual response to his plight. "How in hell am I supposed to live those months?" Chance turned the pockets of his breeches inside out to emphasize that he was indeed destitute.

The shuffle of boots on the wooden floor drew the gambler's attention to Tolbert, who stood and dug into his own pants pockets. "You're not all that broke. I found this in your pockets that night I made you bathe. This'll buy a lot of beans."

The deputy placed a twenty-dollar gold piece in Chance's palm. For a long silent moment the gambler stared at the single coin, trying to contain an anger that threatened to become an exploding rage. "But it won't buy me a weapon or a roof over my head. Hell, this will barely cover the price of a new shirt and a pair of pants."

"You're welcome to the use of a cot back in one of the cells for as long as you like, Pardee said. "It ain't the Beltin Hotel, but it's warm and clean."

Chance swallowed the string of curses that rose in his throat. Like it or not, with only twenty dollars to his name and the unwelcomed prospect of spending months in Beltin, he might have to take the sheriff up on the offer of a cot.

"I think we ought to foot the bill for Doc Henry giving him a going over, too, Glen." This from Tolbert. "He did tangle with a grizzly and got torn up a might."

Pardee nodded. "Least we can do to show our hospitality. Take him over to Doc's then by Ed Norton's store, if he's still a mind to buy those shirt and breeches."

Realizing he wasn't going to get any further concessions from the sheriff, Chance changed his tactics. "What about a telegram? Does Beltin have a telegraph office?"

"What do you think this is—the backwoods?" Pardee stared at him dubiously. "'Course we've got a telegraph office."

"Then do you think the municipality of Beltin would agree to pay for a telegram to New Orleans? I'd like to inform my friends and business associates of the fact that I'm still alive, and have them wire some money to expedite my return to civilization." The gambler found it impossible to keep the sarcasm from his tone. If this town wasn't the backwoods, he didn't know what was.

"Wiring for money won't do you much good," Tolbert said. "The bank doesn't have the funds to cash a draft."

Damn! For a moment the gambler had completely forgotten the robbery that had brought him to Beltin in the first place. "At least I can let my friends know that I'm alive," he answered.

After scratching his neck again for several seconds, the sheriff finally acquiesced. "If you keep the telegram's cost below five dollars, I can handle it from petty cash."

"Agreed," the gambler said with a nod. He then turned to Tolbert. "I believe the sheriff mentioned something about a store where I could buy some new clothes."

The deputy tilted his head toward the jail's door. "We'll visit Doc Henry first."

"Hold your left arm out to your side again, Mr. Sharpe, and lift it as high as you can," the gray-haired, bespectacled physician requested, then stepped back to observe the movement.

Shirtless, Chance sat perched on the edge of the doctor's examination table. He held his left arm straight out then lifted it another forty-five degrees. Stiffness prevented it from going higher.

Doc Henry peered at the gambler over the rims of his glasses. "You can get dressed, Mr. Sharpe."

Chance stood and lifted his tattered shirt from the back of a chair that stood beside the examination table. While he slipped buttons into their holes, he asked, "Well, Doctor, what's the verdict?"

"That you're a lucky man, Mr. Sharpe, a damned lucky man. Either of those wounds would have killed a man with a weaker constitution." The physician walked to a glass-doored cabinet and busily searched shelf after shelf filled with an array of brown, green, and blue bottles. "Both of the wounds have closed themselves, and there's no need for stitches. However, you need to limit your activity until you can build up your strength. At the same time I want you to exercise that arm and side. You have to stretch those muscles or they'll bind on you and leave you half-crippled the rest of your life."

The gambler accepted a blue bottle with a cork stopper that the doctor handed him. "What's this?"

"An ointment I want you to rub on your shoulder and side two or three times a day. It'll keep the skin moist and pliant. Remember, you've got to stretch those muscles. It'll hurt a mite at first, but in the long run, it'll pay off." Doc Henry pulled the spectacles from his nose and dropped them into the breast pocket of his black coat. "I also want you to eat a lot of red meat and viscera, like liver and beef hearts. You lost more than your share of blood; this diet will help build it up again."

The twenty-dollar gold piece in the gambler's pocket might go a long way in the purchase of beans, but it wouldn't last more than a few days on the diet the physician had just prescribed. Chance grimaced; his stay in Beltin grew more bleak with each passing second.

EIGHT

Chance stepped from the general store's back room dressed in a new dark blue woolen shirt and pair of black pants of an equally coarse weave. A smile of amusement hung at the corners of his mouth when he glanced down at the clothing. Both shirt and trousers were a far cry from the expensive, tailored attire to which he was accustomed.

A farmer come into town for store-bought clothes, he mentally pictured himself while he ran a hand beneath the shirt's collar to gain a moment's relief from the prickly fabric. He could easily imagine the stares and jibes he would garner from his friends if he stepped aboard the *Wild Card* in this condition. Both this clothing and the black beard sprouted over cheeks and chin and crawling halfway down his neck would have to go before he resumed his life on the Mississippi.

"Two new shirts and pairs of breeches—that totals four dollars and fifty cents," Ed Norton, the store's owner, said when the gambler approached the counter. "Will there be anything else?"

"Cigars," Chance replied.

The gambler's gaze traveled about the wooden-framed store. Its every nook and cranny was crammed with some item that just possibly might be of use to those who dwelled on the frontier of the Dakota Territory. After his weeks in the wilderness the vast array of foodstuffs and dry goods seemed like an esoteric collection of exotic treasures from around the world.

"Best cigars in Beltin." Norton grinned widely as he lifted a wooden box from a shelf behind him. He opened the lid to display a neat row of green-leafed cigars. "Two for a nickel. How many would you like?"

The fat stogies weren't his preferred long, slim, black sabers, but the gambler didn't complain. Even cheap tobacco would taste good after his long absence from a cigar. "Fifty cents worth, Mr. Norton."

"That brings your total to five dollars," the store owner said. "See anything else you need?"

Chance's eyes shifted around the store. He felt like a child with a nickel in his pocket faced with the decision of whether to splurge his fortune on licorice ropes, peppermint sticks, or rock candy. For a moment he studied a wooden-handled razor and the two-dollar price tag on it. His attention then shifted to a glass display case that contained five revolvers. A .44 caliber Remington like his own on the *Wild Card* looked the most promising of the handguns, but its price was far too prohibited for a man with only fifteen dollars remaining to his name.

"I believe that will be all for the moment," the gambler finally answered with the realization that he'd have to maintain a tight rein on his purse strings until he found a source of income in this backwoods metropolis.

Norton took the twenty-dollar gold piece and returned the gambler fifteen dollars in change. "We appreciate your business. I noticed you eyeing that Remington in the case. Would you like for me to put it aside for you for a couple of days?"

"A tempting proposal, Mr. Norton, but I believe it's above my means for the foreseeable future. Thank you anyway." Chance's right hand rose to tip the brim of his hat, finding only air. He smiled in chagrin. A hat was another item that he had to forego purchasing for the time being.

Donning his ripped coat, the gambler stuffed the twine-bound, brown-paper package containing his change of clothing beneath his left arm. With a nod to John Tolbert, who had been waiting behind him, he headed toward the store's front door. "Now, where's that telegraph office?"

"At the end of Main Street." The deputy tilted his head to the right. "There's a cobbler shop on the way. Olsen usually sticks to making and repairing boots, but he might be able to do something about patching that coat."

Chance glanced at the ripped shoulder and side of his coat. He shrugged. "It's a mite breezy, but for now I don't think I can afford the price of thread."

"It'll be on me," the deputy answered, pointing the gambler toward the bootmaker's store front.

Chance's right eyebrow arched in question. "Not feeling a touch of guilt, are you, Deputy?"

"Me?" Tolbert's shoulders shifted as though the man was uncomfortable. "Just trying to help out a soul who's down on his luck, that's all."

"Certainly," Chance answered with an amused smile. Whether he would admit it or not, the lawman was attempting to make amends for his mistake. The gambler didn't mind—just wished that it were more. Beltin was a long way from the Missouri River.

Inside the cobbler's shop a balding man wearing a green-tinted eye-shade examined the torn coat, "mmm"ed to himself for several seconds, nodded, then in a German accent proclaimed that the best he could do was patch the ripped leather. When Chance gave his approval for the repair, the cobbler told him to pick up the coat that afternoon.

In spite of the rough fabric pricking at the back of his neck, the gambler was grateful for the woolen shirt. Although no snow lay on the ground, winter was in the Dakota air. He rubbed briskly at his arms when he and Tolbert returned to the street.

"Don't let Glen mislead you," the deputy said while they walked toward a yellow and black shingle that marked the telegraph office. "There should be a wagon heading east within a week or two. Snow won't get bad enough to stop wagons until late December."

Chance only half listened to the lawman. His gaze fell upon a whitewashed wooden building with a sign over its door that read THE HOTEL BELTIN. More important was a business establishment built directly beside the hotel. Its red sign with gold letters brazenly proclaimed THE GOLDEN EAGLE SALOON. Smaller signs painted in the same red and gold ran down each sides of its double-doored entrance. These listed the enticements to be found inside. The gambler quickly scanned a claim of "dancing girls, beer, and hard spirits," his attention focusing on the games of chance one could partake of within. Poker headed a list that included roulette, dice, and the ever popular and so easy to rig game of Keno.

". . . Ed Norton usually has a wagon heading east every few weeks." Tolbert's words wedged inside the gambler's thoughts as the two men stepped inside the telegraph office.

It took five minutes for Chance to jot down a brief message to his attorney and friend Philip Duwayne in New Orleans, explaining that he was alive and well and unavoidably detained in Beltin. After the deputy handed the telegraph operator three dollars, the man immediately sat before the key and fired off the message in a clicking electronic burst of dots and dashes. He then assured the two that the message would be relayed to New Orleans within twenty-four hours.

"The sheriff has lunch brought into the jail from Nellie's Café each day. There'll be enough for another mouth," Tolbert said awkwardly, inviting the gambler back to the jail for a meal.

Chance stopped and looked toward the jail before his eyes traveled to the Golden Eagle Saloon with its promise of gaming tables painted in gaudy red and gold. The weight of the fifteen dollars in pocket was less than a secure sensation.

"I might have to take you up on that offer tonight," the gambler answered Tolbert. "That is, if it's still open?"

The deputy's gaze moved to the saloon and hung there a moment. A dubious expression furrowed the lawman's brow when he turned back to Chance. "For a man with only fifteen dollars to his name, it seems to me you're taking an awfully big risk."

Chance shrugged. "Risk is a gambler's stock and trade." Beltin's bank might have been cleaned out by Martin Ranson, but if there was a spare dollar to be found in this town, the gambler knew he'd find it in the Golden Eagle. No matter how many notches men had to pull in their belts in hard times, they always seemed to find the finances to support their vices. Chance didn't expect the situation was any different on the Dakota frontier.

"Sheriff Pardee might not take kindly to feeding a man who blew what money he had shooting craps," Tolbert said. "But if you need a meal tonight, I'll see that you get one."

"I've no intention of blowing my bankroll—or of shooting craps," the gambler replied as he started toward the saloon. "Poker's my game."

"Good luck, Chance," the deputy called after him.

Chance stopped and glanced back over a shoulder. "I think that I prefer Sharpe. If you start calling me by my first name, you might get the idea that we're friends."

Surprise washed over Tolbert's face and then recognition as he realized the gambler had just thrown his own words back at him. Leaving the lawman standing in the middle of the street, Chance entered the Golden Eagle Saloon to ply his chosen profession.

NINE

Chance chewed on the stubby remains of the second "two fer" he had smoked his way through in the past six hours while he eyed the three queens and pair of deuces in his hand. Closing the cards, he placed them on the green-felt-covered table, took a blue chip from the stack in front of him, and tossed it atop the bright array of white and red chips at the center of the table.

The gambler's steel blue gaze lifted to the other four players seated at the game. He knew none of their names, and their faces varied little from the procession of men who had taken seats at the game throughout the long afternoon. Each of the four glanced at the blue chip then carefully studied his hand a second time.

"Too rich for my blood!" A man in faded overalls on Chance's left tossed in his cards."

"I call," a man in a worn brown suit said as he added a blue chip to the pot and cast a suspicious glance in the gambler's direction.

"I'll stay." This from a silver-haired gentleman in a natty black suit and tie, who Chance vaguely remembered as being introduced as the proprietor of the Hotel Beltin.

"And I'll call." The last man at the table plopped a wooden blue chip into the pot. He then looked at Chance. "What's your hand look like, friend?"

"Three ladies"—Chance fanned his five cards face up on the table—"and a pair of deuces."

"Beats the hell out of my two pair," brown suit threw down his cards with a grunt of disgust.

The silver-haired gentleman merely folded without comment and began to count the chips that remained before him. The final player cursed his own parentage when he tossed down three kings partnered with a five of spades and a seven of hearts. "Damnation! I was certain that I had you that time!"

Chance raked in the pot and separated the colored chips into their correct stacks beside him. Gathering the cards, he began to shuffle. "Five card draw, no wild cards, and jacks or better to open."

"Gentlemen"—the bartender approached the table—"time to cash in your chips. It's five to seven, and you ain't got time for another hand."

The gambler looked up; his right eyebrow arched high in question.

The bartender shrugged apologetically. "Sorry, but them's the new rules ever since the bank was robbed. At seven each night the price of chips doubles. You have to go to the cage, cash in, and buy new chips if you want to continue to play."

"Just as well," overalls said while he pushed from the table. "I should've been home for supper two hours ago. I'll be lucky if Sarah Lou don't take a fry pan to me."

"Evening repast sounds exceptional," the silver-haired gentleman agreed as he and the two others rose and walked to the cashier's cage with their chips.

"Can I reserve a chair for the evening game?" Chance inquired when the bartender started to leave.

The man grinned and chuckled. "Wouldn't worry none about fighting for a chair. Cash in your chips and come back to the table. You'll be lucky to draw enough men for a game. Things have been a mite tight since Martin Ranson cleaned out the bank."

The gambler nodded his thanks. Scrapping his chips from the table, he gave them a quick tally—thirty dollars!

He smiled with the realization that he had doubled his funds. *Not a bad afternoon.*

On its face, winning a mere fifteen dollars in six hours didn't appear to be a major feat. However, when one considered that chips were sold for a nickel, a dime, and a quarter, it assumed the proportion of a Herculean task.

Doubling the cost of the chips for the evening play would do little to enhance the possibility of royal pots, Chance realized while he cashed in his chips and repurchased them at the higher night rate. Apparently John Tolbert hadn't been exaggerating when he said the bank robbery had left everyone in town broke.

With half the number of his original chips in his hands, Chance left the cashier's cage and returned to the now empty poker table. Refusing to be disheartened by the lack of challengers, he pulled another of the cheap cigars from his shirt pocket, lit it, and let his eyes play over the saloon.

The Golden Eagle was surprisingly luxurious for a frontier establishment of its ilk. The bar was finished and polished complete with brass foot rail and spittoons. Hung over the bar, behind a wide assortment of liquor bottles and neatly stacked pyramids of glasses and mugs, ran a two-sectioned mirror, at least ten feet long.

Like the bar, the Golden Eagle's tables and chairs were finished and varnished rather than rough-hewn pieces of furniture. The same could be said of the walls and the floor, which seemed to be very well swept and clean.

A single door on the saloon's right wall led directly into the lobby of the Hotel Beltin, which left the gambler to believe both establishments were controlled by the same man. Inside the lobby, Chance discerned a black and white sign that proclaimed a haircut, shave, and hot bath all could be had for a mere fifty cents. Running his right hand over the thick black beard covering his cheeks and chin, the gambler promised himself to partake of the offer before the night was through—if his luck continued!

The rinky-tink notes of an upright piano drew Chance's attention to the back of the saloon. There a piano player, seated at his instrument beside a small curtained stage, let his fingers lightly dance across the keys. Another musician perched on a stool beside him and began to tune the strings of a battered-looking five-string banjo. Within two minutes the two were in tune and producing a lively version of "Sweet Betsy from Pike."

Chance's recollection of the "dancing girls" the sign outside the Golden Eagle had promised was interrupted by the silver-haired gentleman he had played with that afternoon. The man reintroduced himself as Charles Lafare, and confirmed Chance's memory as being the hotel's proprietor, although Lafare made no mention of owning the saloon. Likewise, Chance gave no indication of his true profession as he repeated his name to the hotel owner. Pickings were slim enough in Beltin as it was; there was no reason to scare off the only man willing to take a seat at the table.

The two passed the next fifteen minutes with the usual small talk about the weather and the slow crowd patronizing the Golden Eagle tonight. They bordered on running out of things to say before two more men took the vacant chairs at the table. Doc Henry, Chance had met earlier. The fourth man was a Harrison Clive, an unlikely name for Beltin's blacksmith.

While his fellow players anted their dime white chips, Chance waved for a fresh deck from the bar, shuffled the cards, and placed them at the center of the table. The cut won Clive the deal and his announced game of seven-card stud; three tens won Chance a dollar pot. He added another two dollars when the deal was passed to him on a pair of kings in five card draw. Four fives increased his bankroll to thirty-five dollars on the next hand.

"People!" the piano player called out as the banjo player finished a rendition of "Cumberland Gap." "For your entertainment and enjoyment, the Golden Eagle is proud to present the golden voice of Miss Marilee Dupree."

Chance paid no attention to the lackluster introduction and continued to shuffle the deck. However, every other head in the saloon turned to the small stage. Anticipation lit the Golden Eagle's patrons' faces as the multicolored curtain opened to reveal a busty blond in a silken gown of forest green.

The enticing image of feminine beauty at the corner of his eye was enough to momentarily push thoughts of poker from the gambler's mind. Afterall, there was no need to deal the cards when his four companions' minds wandered elsewhere. Like every other man in the saloon, he lifted his head and devoted his full attention to Marilee Dupree as she began to sing a medley of Stephen Foster songs.

There was no doubting why the saloon's patrons so intensely ogled the slender, young woman who gracefully stepped down two steps to the Golden Eagle's floor and began to wander among the tables while she sang. Luxurious blond tresses, like fine strands of frosted gold, cascaded over the singer's ivory shoulders, inviting longing, male eyes to caress the tantalizing alluring valley of cleavage revealed by the wide V of her plunging neckline. With each breath she took, Marilee Dupree exposed a full, rounded expanse of satiny smooth flesh.

Equally provocative was the European design of the rich green gown. A far cry from the widely flaring skirts with their layer upon layer of ruffles and petticoats worn by Southern belles before the war, the fabric of this gown clung to Marilee's hips and hinted at the supple contours of coltishly long legs beneath. The clinging tightness of the gown also emphasized the movement of her definitely womanly buttocks with each step she took.

There were no wild catcalls as she sang. Nor did the men's arms snake out to ensnare the young singer's waspishly slender waist. The Golden Eagle's patrons simply stared, mesmerized by Marilee Dupree's regal beauty.

Chance stared, too, but with mouth wide and jaw sagging in shock!

When he managed to find his voice, he whispered to Doc Henry, "What did they say her name was?"

"Marilee Dupree," the physician replied, his eyes never leaving the seductive blond. "She came to town about six months ago. Every man in Beltin would give his right arm to call her his—me included! And damn the missus and my three daughters!"

Chance looked back at the singer, unable to recover from the surprise of finding *her* here. He didn't know the name Marilee Dupree, but he most definitely knew the woman, who sported yet another in a long line of identities.

Andrews had been her name when he had first met her aboard the *Wild Card* a few days after his release from the army. She had also been a singer aboard the sidewheeler then. It had taken only one glance into Marilee's emerald green eyes to ignite lusty fantasies in the gambler's mind.

After Chance had won the riverboat from its owner, Tate Browder, Marilee had remained aboard the steamer entertaining the paddlewheeler's passengers with her songs at dinner and fulfilling the boat's new owner's fantasies during the night.

A pleased smile moved over the gambler's lips while he recalled the summery warmth of her skin beneath his exploring hands, the womanly fragrance of her body as they sank atop his bed, the uninhibited passion when she surrendered herself to his desire. Had all gone to his mental plans, Marilee Andrews might now be Marilee Sharpe, a regal queen aboard the *Wild Card*.

Chance's smile faded as other memories wedged inside his head. There was another side of Marilee Andrews that had revealed itself when he neared New Orleans, intent on legally filing title to his newly won riverboat—a brutally cruel side akin to a black widow.

Marilee Andrews, it turned out, was in fact Marilee Browder, daughter of the man he had won the *Wild Card* from. And a very loyal daughter at that! *Especially with a reward of ten thousand dollars to secure that loyalty,* Chance recalled.

While Browder employed cutthroats and river pirates to retake the paddlewheeler from its new owner, Marilee employed her own wiles to the same ends. Her efforts were spurred on by the ten thousand her father had promised if she were successful. That little twist had eluded the gambler until he found himself bound hand and foot in a New Orleans warehouse, the guest of Marilee and a gorilla-sized thug who methodically worked Chance over with his fists while the blond watched every punishing blow.

Their intent had been to retrieve the *Wild Card*'s title before Chance filed it at the New Orleans courthouse. They failed. Barely conscious from his repeated beatings, the gambler managed to escape. In a final confrontation between Browder and the crew of another riverboat, Browder was killed and Marilee captured.

Chance had planned to turn the treacherous blond over to the New Orleans authorities when the *Wild Card* docked in the Crescent City. Only Marilee had escaped from her stateroom cell, leaving a note behind for the gambler. Even now, he could recall every word formed by her graceful hand.

> A son cannot be held accountable for the sins of the father. Can a daughter? Nor can that daughter place blame on a man who killed to defend what was rightfully his, Chance. We, you and I, simply did what was required of us.
>
> Had times and situations been different when we met, perhaps . . .

The remainder of that line had been scratched through so heavily that the gambler had been unable to make out her words. But there had been a final paragraph to the note:

> Surely, you understand why I cannot remain aboard the *New Moon* and face the authorities who wait in New Orleans. Perhaps in the not-so-distant future we will meet again under more favorable circumstances. I hope you look forward to that day as I do, Chance.

New Moon, he hadn't thought of the *Wild Card*'s original name in months. He wished he could say the same for Marilee Browder, or Dupree as the case now was. In spite of the way she had betrayed him, Chance had felt no animosity toward the blond, only regret that circumstances had stood between them. A woman like Marilee was hard, if not impossible, to forget!

Chance's cool blue eyes followed her every movement as she continued to wind between the Golden Eagle's tables. *Perhaps in the not-so-distant future we will meet again under more favorable circumstances. I hope you look forward to that day as I do, Chance.* The last two lines of her parting note echoed in his mind while the beautiful young singer worked close to his table. He had never openly admitted it to himself—until now—he *had* looked forward to the day they might meet again.

That day has come! Anticipation coursed through the gambler when Marilee stepped beside the green-felt–covered poker table. Her gemlike emerald eyes met the faces of his companions one by one, then alighted on him and hung there for a full eight bars of her song.

Again Chance's jaw sagged. There was no flicker of recognition on her beautiful features, no hint that she had ever seen him before. Why?

Bewildered, the gambler sank back into his chair, his anticipation as deflated as his ego. He scratched at his heavy beard while Marilee climbed back to the stage and concluded the medley.

Chance's fingertips halted, and a smile uplifted the corners of his mouth as he resumed stroking the thick forest of facial hair. It was no wonder Marilee had not recognized him. Dressed as he was, and his face hidden beneath a beard, his own two brothers wouldn't have recognized him.

A soft, longing sigh drew the gambler's gaze to Doc Henry when the curtain closed to end Marilee's performance. The physician's head slowly moved from side to side. "Since the only thing anyone of us at this table is going to have the pleasure of playing with this night is these cards, we might as well get on with it."

Chance smiled with amusement while he reshuffled the cards and dealt the next hand. The tightness of his groin was testimony to Marilee's still powerful effect on him. If his luck held, he hoped to prove Doc wrong before the night grew too old.

"Pour it over my head, Willard," Chance directed the bath's attendant as the man approached the steaming bathtub with another wooden bucket of hot water.

The middle-aged man did as told. The cascading water washed the thick lather from the gambler's freshly cut hair.

"If I had a singing voice, I'd belt out a tune." Chance shook his head, sending a spray of water droplets through the air. "Since I couldn't carry a tune in that bucket, I'll spare your ears, Willard."

The attendant smiled politely while he tidily arranged a stack of white towels on a wooden bench beside the tub.

The temptation was to sink chin deep in the hot water and soak for an hour or three. Chance resisted that urge. Whistling a nameless tune, he pushed from the steaming water and briskly toweled himself dry. The hot bath had worked wonders. Even his shoulder and side seemed to have lost some of their stiffness.

All in all, it's been a good day, he grudgingly admitted to himself while he dressed. In spite of being stranded in Nowhere, Dakota, he had been cleared of a bank robbery and murder. And his pockets now contained a hundred dollars. *That's after paying for a hot meal of steak and potatoes.* He rubbed his full belly, remembering when a diet of raw fish and crawdads had been his only fare.

Leaving a dollar for Willard's services, Chance walked from the bathhouse built behind the Hotel Beltin and reentered the lobby. Fifty cents paid to the clerk bought him a room for the night. He accepted the key and directions to Room 25 on the second floor.

Although he climbed the stairway to the hotel's second level, Room 25 was not his destination. Chance had ended his evening at the poker table the moment Marilee had concluded her final performance of the night. Discreetly he had followed the blond into the hotel, watching her enter Room 20 before he arranged for the advertised haircut, shave, and bath. Now that he had partaken of all three, he planned to pay a beautiful songbird a little visit.

He reached a door with the number 20 painted on the wood in white and lightly rapped it with his knuckles.

"Just a moment," Marilee called out.

Chance heard the shuffle of footsteps within, then the click of a lock being slipped from its niche. In the next instant the door opened.

"Is there . . ." Marilee's words died in a startled gasp. Her emerald eyes flew wide in fear. "Chance? Chance Sharpe?"

TEN

Marilee's face paled when the identity of her unexpected caller penetrated. Her long, graceful fingers trembled as they clutched the top of the black lace dressing robe she wore. She swallowed hard with uncertainty.

"Aren't you going to invite me in?" A wry smile edged over Chance's lips. He could easily guess what thoughts rushed through the singer's head at this moment. And whatever her imagination created wasn't enough retribution for what she had done to him in New Orleans. "This isn't the greeting I expected, Marilee. After all, we are old friends—once, even more. I thought that you looked forward to the day we'd meet again? At least, that's what you said in the note you left."

"Chance . . ." His name came from her quivering lips again. Those emerald eyes remained wide and round. "Chance . . ."

In spite of his original intentions of simply renewing his acquaintance with this enticing blond, Chance found himself savoring the moment. She deserved every dark image that flooded her mind as a reminder of each punishing blow he had endured inside that New Orleans warehouse.

"Well, if you aren't going to invite me in," he said, "I guess that I'll just have to invite myself."

Like a frightened rabbit, Marilee backstepped, still clutching her robe close. The gambler stepped inside the hotel room, closed the door behind him, and slid the lock into its niche with a sharp click.

"Chance," she started again in an attempt to regain her composure. She failed miserably. Her voice quavered and the frosty strands of her hair trembled. "Chance . . . I . . . how did . . . where . . . I didn't expect . . ."

Without the batting of an eye to announce his intentions, Chance crossed the distance separating them in a single stride. His arms snaked out and locked around her slender waist, crushing her diminutive body to him.

"Oh!" a piteous whimper of obvious terror pushed from the depths of her throat.

His hold secure with his right arm, the gambler reached up with his left hand and locked his fingers into her frosty gold tresses. Ignoring her comfort, he yanked back to force her face upward so that she stared directly into his eyes. In the next instant he leaned forward; his mouth covered her trembling lips.

"Oh!" Another whimper rose from her throat.

And parted her lips to allow his tongue to thrust deeply into the sweetness of her mouth.

"Ooohhh!" A third whimper of distress melted into a soft moan of pleasant surprise and then into a pleasured, "Mmmmmmmm."

Marilee's hands released the crushed fabric beneath her fingers and encircled Chance's waist. The polished nails of those fingers nipped at his back while her tongue passionately welcomed his.

Only when his left hand unwove from the strands of her hair did the gambler's lips release hers. For long silent moments he gazed down, tracing the classic beauty of her oval face, losing himself in the green of her eyes that now sparkled with smoldering fire rather than fear, a fire that he remembered oh so well. Although she deserved every horrifying image of brutal revenge her mind had conjured but seconds ago, it wasn't what he wanted—

she was what he wanted! And until this moment, he hadn't realized how much.

Down the gentle arch of her back his hands traveled, stopping only when his palms cupped the rounded contours of her buttocks. A hint of a smile touched the natural redness of her lips when he pulled her closer. As their mouths met again, it was she who rose on her tiptoes, stretching to him. Her tongue taunted at his lips then playfully danced into his mouth. All the while his fingers kneaded the taunt cheeks of her hindquarters so that the mound of her pelvis pressed firmly against his own growing need.

Flames of desire burned in her eyes when their lips parted a second time. Her voice softened to a whisper when she said, "This wasn't the greeting I expected from—"

He cut her short with another kiss. Her body trembled beneath his stroking palms. However, those tiny flesh tremors no longer had anything to do with fear!

"I *do* like the way you make an old friend feel welcome, Chance Sharpe." The tone of her voice changed once again; this time to a dreamy drunkenness.

His hands rose from her buttocks and grasped her waist. Gently he eased her warmth from him so that his eyes could leisurely caress every inch of her. "I haven't finished saying hello."

He found the knotted sash of the black lace draped over her body and gave it a quick tug. Marilee shivered as the front of the robe fell open. For an instant Chance's gaze probed shadowy hints of satiny flesh revealed by the slightly parted fabric. Down the deep valley separating her voluptuous breasts, over the fluttering flatness of her stomach to the soft triangle of pale blond down bushed between the sleekness of her thighs.

While she stood watching him, he lifted both hands and tucked them inside the lace. Slowly, as though he were some collector undraping a priceless work of art, he eased the robe from her shoulders. Downward it flowed, over her arms and then to the floor, where it gathered about her ankles like midnight mist.

"Beautiful." The single word worked from his lips as he drank in her unashamed nakedness.

She was beautiful, more beautiful than he remembered. *And dangerous,* he reminded himself. And in the next pounding of his heart cast caution to the wind. *Danger be damned!*

When he came to her again, it was to sweep her into his arms and carry her to the bed, where he gently placed her. The creamy mounds of her heavy breasts heaved in disappointment when he stepped back to work the buttons of his shirt from their holes.

If there had been fires of desire in her deep green eyes before, hunger now dwelled in those jewellike orbs as the gambler tugged off his shirt, tossed it aside, then skinned down his breeches to display the full measure of his arousal. The pink tip of her tongue flicked moistly at her lips as he stood naked above her. Her arms rose and her long coltish legs opened, both beckoning him to her.

He didn't refuse the invitation. He came to her, sliding atop the summery warmth of her body. He mentally smiled. His own bath had been well timed; Marilee had apparently just stepped from her own when he had arrived at her door. The fresh smell of soap with a hint of talc wafted in his nostrils when his mouth covered hers once again. And beneath the aromas of soap and talc lay the undeniable scent of a woman!

When Chance's lips left her mouth, they traveled on a direct course down her gracefully arching neck toward the swollen mounds of her breasts. A destination his hands reached first! With decided relish, his fingers kneaded into the pliant flesh of those twin billowy mountains. Soft moans trembled from Marilee's lips while her head lolled from side to side.

Those moans deepened with an equal amount of pleasure as his lips and tongue found one of the dark nubbins perched high atop her breasts. In taunting circles, his tongue cajoled that delightful button until it swelled to a ripe cherry of desire. Then he moved on to the next.

All the while his hands stroked and caressed, soaking in the luxury of her body. Abandoning the sleek domes of her breasts, his fingertips traced along her sides to explore the suppleness of her thighs before working inward to the silky down covering her womanly knoll.

Nor were her hands idle. Her fingertips strolled over the wide expanse of his muscular back, tentatively brushing the knotted scars of bullet and knife he had garnered as mementoes from a life along the Mississippi and the long years of the Civil War. Down her hands eased, finding his buttocks to squeeze them as he had done to hers. Then, imitating his action, she slipped a hand between their bodies and grasped his length.

Chance needed no other urging to tell him the time of their union had arrived. His hips arched upward then eased down and forward. Her guiding fingers directed him into the liquid warmth of her body. A moan of satisfaction softly came from her lips.

For moments he just lay there bathing in the marvelous feel of her. A shudder of desire ran through her diminutive form when at last he began to move. Gently at first, his hips undulated while his palms crept upward to once more cup the firm demi-globes of her breasts.

Her mouth found his, and her tongue thrust deeply toward his throat while her pelvis met the rhythm he set. In slow, gyrating circles she worked about him, first releasing him then drawing him deeper into the intimate shelter of her willing body.

Doing his damnedest to ignore the molten fire that swelled within him, he read each and every quake of need that tremored through the magnificent woman beneath him. With lips, tongue, and fingertips he stoked the fires of lust, fanning her urgency to match his own.

Her signs of delight gave way to deep-throated moans of pleasure unleashed. Quake after shuddering quake raced through her body as she clenched at his back, fingernails biting into his flesh. Her lust realized, his hips thrust downward one last time, and he allowed the flood within his body to flow forth like liquid fire.

Together they held each other while their hands and fingertips soothed and caressed their sweat-sheened bodies. Tenderly their lips moved over their necks and faces in a language far older than the first verbal utterings of man. Only when his own body gave up the last of its adamant strength did he ease from her. Enfolding her in his arms, he drew her close so that their bodies pressed front to back like living spoons.

For the first time in weeks, Chance felt alive. Not even the usual drowsiness that settles over a man after lovemaking plagued him. The fragrance of her hair in his nostrils, he lay there enjoying how snugly the contours of their bodies matched one another. His senses seemed more alive than they had since the *Wild Card* had begun its trip up the Big Muddy. His palms and fingertips could feel the gentling of Marilee's heartbeat as her pulse gradually returned to normal. His ears heard the rhythm of her breathing, which had come fast and sharp such a short time before, shallow with every breath she drew. His eyes detected subtle nuances in the flickering golden light from a whale oil lamp that washed the hotel room in its soft glow.

A sudden shiver that ran through Marilee's nakedness was a harsh incongruity to the deep-seeded satisfaction that overflowed every cell of his body. Pushing up on an elbow, he lightly kissed her bare shoulder. "Something wrong?"

"Just getting a bit cold." Her eyes rolled up to him, and she smiled. "I was about to light a fire when you knocked at the door. After that, I completely forgot about the fireplace."

Kissing her forehead, Chance eased his arm from beneath her side and slipped from the bed. "Get under the covers, and I'll build a fire."

Marilee gave him no argument, shivering louder when her nakedness touched the cool sheets. "Hurry. It's warmer with two in here."

The gambler grinned while he carefully built a pile of kindling, placed a log atop it, then lit it with a match. Once he was certain the log had caught fire, he trotted to the bed. The lovely blond tossed back the covers and welcomed him into the warmth of her waiting embrace.

"Better?"

"Better," she answered with a nod and a kiss. However, when their lips eased apart, her brow furrowed.

"Now there *is* something wrong," Chance said.

"Not wrong, just wondering." Marilee bit at her lower lip while her eyes rolled back up to study the rugged features of his face.

"Wondering about what?" He kissed the fingertips that rose to lightly trace over his cheek.

"Why you're here," she answered. "As much as I'd like to believe that you spent nearly a year tracking me down and followed me here to Beltin, I'm not that naive. I don't believe there's ever been a woman in your life that meant that much to you, Chance."

He shrugged and let his lips brush hers. "There was once. Trouble was, I was the naive one. I didn't even realize that she was after my riverboat and not me until she had a hired tough try to kill me in a New Orleans warehouse."

She stiffened beside him but didn't pull away. "After what just happened between us, I had the impression that you had forgiven me that."

"Forgiven, yes," he said. "But forgetting that someone tried to have you beaten to a pulp is a bit more difficult. I'm still working on that."

Her eyes lowered, and she nodded in silent acceptance of his reproach. "If you give me the time, I'll try to make that up to you. You must remember that the man you were facing was my father. I couldn't have gone against him."

"Or the ten thousand he promised you for the *New Moon*'s title." Chance almost regretted the words as he uttered them—almost, but not quite. There was no reason to begin this fresh start between them on a lie.

"Or the ten thousand," she admitted. "I won't say it didn't influence me. With that money I would have been free of my father. That was a hard fact to ignore."

He let the comment slide by, unable to recall any mention of difficulties between Tate Browder and his daughter until this moment.

"What about the *New Moon?*" Marilee looked up at him again. "I remember you were considering selling her once you got her to New Orleans."

"She's called the *Wild Card* now," he answered, then paused and arched an eyebrow. "Why? Does a paddle-wheeler still mean that much to you?"

"That one does." Marilee's voice lowered. "It separated me from the only man that I've ever truly cared about."

She caught him off guard. He was unprepared for such an admission. If it *was* that, and not merely words meant to sway him. As he had thought before, she was dangerous. It would be shear stupidity to underestimate that danger especially if he stood between something she wanted. He had made that mistake once and had no intention of repeating it.

Apparently sensing his uneasiness, she quickly changed the subject. "You still haven't told me what brought you to this portion of the Dakota Territory."

"A bear and a lynch mob," he answered with a playful grin.

Marilee lightly touched the healing wounds on his left shoulder and right side. "A bear would explain these, but I don't understand the lynch mob."

"I guess you couldn't catagorize five men out to hang me a mob, but I don't think you could call them friendly, either." Backtracking to the *Wild Card*'s rotted meat supplies, he recounted the series of misadventures that had resulted in his unexpected stay in Beltin. He concluded by mentioning that he had caught all three of her performances in the Golden Eagle that night.

"You were in the saloon?" A startled expression crossed the delicate features of her face. Then she smiled as her arms wrapped about his waist and her fingers lightly stroked over his buttocks. "Of course! You were the man at the poker table—the one with the black beard and the unruly hair. I knew there was something familiar about that face, but I couldn't put my finger on it."

"I prefer your fingers exactly where they are at the moment, thank you very much!" He kissed her and pulled her nakedness closer.

"I'm willing to wager that I can think of even a better spot for my fingers." Her long eyelashes batted coyly while one of her hands wiggled between them to prove she knew exactly what she was talking about.

"Keep that up, lady, and it will be tomorrow morning before I find out how you ended up in this godforsaken town." One of his own hands moved from her back to busy a sleeping nipple. She shivered with unashamed relish as her flesh awoke and swelled beneath his gentle ministrations.

"Are you certain that you wouldn't rather wait until morning?" She tightened her grip on him as though making sure he knew that she had things other than recounting recent histories on her mind. To emphasize the point, her lips lifted to cover his.

An old Indian saying wedged itself inside Chance's mind—"The night is for sleeping or making love. Talk is for the light of day."

Marilee's mouth slipped from his and began to taunt its way downward over his chest and stomach. By the time she had captured him between her lips, he had completely forgotten what it was he wanted to talk about.

ELEVEN

Marilee's head rested in the hollow of Chance's shoulder while he lay on his back. The gentle flow of her breath tickled its way through the dark forest of hair sprouted on his chest. Far from an irritating sensation, he enjoyed it the way he relished the satiny feel of her nakedness pressed warmly along his length. The young singer had been the first woman to enter his life after the War Between the States; it was good to have her back.

"Damn!" The soft curse pushed from Marilee's lips in a disgusted gust as she suddenly rose to an elbow and stared to the room's windows. "It's snowing."

Chance glanced to his right. A light flurry of powdery white drifted through the glow cast by the few lights that still burned in Beltin. "Nothing to worry about. We're warm and cozy right where we are."

She looked at him with a sad little smile and softly kissed his lips. "A winter in Beltin might not be that bad with you here. But you have no intention of staying, do you?"

"I'd planned to head back to the Missouri at the first chance I got," he answered, repeating what he had said earlier. "Now I'm not so certain."

"And I'd planned to be on my way to California before the first snow." She sank back to the pillow of his right shoulder.

"You could come back to the river with me," he suggested while his left hand gently stroked the frosty gold of her long tresses.

"I don't believe that would be wise, at least for another year or three. My father was Tate Browder, remember? The authorities would be quite happy to see me locked behind bars for the rest of my life, if they couldn't get my neck into a noose." She snuggled back against his side. He sensed a tenseness to her body that hadn't been there a moment ago.

"No charges were ever filed against you," he assured her.

"Daddy dear killed quite a few men trying to get the *New Moon* back from you. Since I was working with him and my name is Browder, I'm certain the law would find a way to charge me with his crimes." Her head moved from side to side, rejecting his proposal of returning to the river.

Chance lay silently for several minutes, holding her closely, his memories replaying the bloody attacks on the *Wild Card* Tate Browder had led. His mind then moved to that morning in New Orleans when Marilee's note had been discovered in her empty stateroom. "I still don't know how you managed to escape your room with two men guarding it."

She pushed to an elbow again, looked down on him, grinned, and chuckled. "And I'd be a fool for letting the cat out of the bag, wouldn't I? Who knows when you'll take me as your prisoner again, Chance."

"I prefer you this way." He returned her grin while his palms caressed the smoothness of her back. "Where did you go?"

"Two hours before the *New Moon* pulled into New Orleans, I jumped ship with what clothes I could stuff into a small valise and two hundred dollars I had tucked away for just that sort of emergency," she began.

Marilee then recounted making her way to Shreveport, Louisiana, where she joined a showboat using the name Marilyn Waite. "It took a little dye, and I was a redhead. The troupe made it all the way to St. Louis before creditors caught up with the boat's owner and confiscated his paddlewheeler."

With a long sigh, she once more returned to his shoulder. She stared into space as she told of the month without work that passed before she found a spot on a smaller showboat that ran the Missouri River.

"That's when I started using the name Marilee Dupree. To be honest, I just couldn't get used to being called Marilyn," she said. "I was doing fairly well until we reached Fargo. A roustabout on another steamer, who had worked for my father, recognized me in spite of the red hair."

The man threatened to expose her to the authorities unless he received the princely sum of five hundred dollars to keep his lips sealed. "That's when I realized the river would never be safe for me. I promised to meet the roustabout the next day with his money, then caught the first coach I could find heading west."

"Beltin isn't California," Chance said. "Why'd you stop here?"

"My money ran out," she answered simply. "It takes a thousand dollars to purchase a rig and buy into a wagon train heading west. I had ten dollars in my purse when I arrived here. If Mr. Lafare hadn't hired me as a singer in the Golden Eagle, I'd probably be taking in washing right now just to stay alive."

The gambler mentally smiled at the conclusion to her hard-luck tale. With her beauty Marilee would never be reduced to taking in laundry—that was one thing he was certain of—no matter how desperate her circumstances.

"How short of the thousand are you?" he asked.

She sighed again. "I have a hundred hidden away. Wouldn't care to loan me a few hundred, would you?"

He laughed and outlined his own miserable financial situation. Marilee found no humor in his predicament. In all honesty, neither did Chance. Although, the hundred nestled in his pants on the floor did ease his mind somewhat. "Who knows, I might hit a winning streak and rake in enough for both of us."

"Not likely. At least not in Beltin." She yawned sleepily and nestled against his shoulder. "There's barely two pennies to rub together in this town after Martin Ranson robbed the bank."

"It might be tight, but the well hasn't gone dry. I didn't do too bad today at the poker table," he replied. "It's just a matter of keeping our hopes up."

Marilee didn't answer. Her breathing came soft and shallow in the gentle rhythm of sleep.

The gambler smiled, closed his eyes, and within minutes drifted into restful dreams.

Marilee moaned softly and rolled herself in the blankets when Chance slipped from the bed. He stared from a window to Beltin's streets below. The same powdery snow that had begun last night still fell, melting as it hit the ground and turning the dirt streets to mud.

The gambler glanced upward. The gray overcast sky gave no hint to the time. The hands of a clock atop Marilee's dresser pointed straight up noon. It was later than he had realized. But then the night had been a long and pleasurable one.

Grabbing his clothes from where they lay scattered over the floor, he dressed, placed another log on the dwindling fire, and quietly eased from the hotel room, leaving the singer alone with her dreams. Downstairs he gave the interior of the Golden Eagle a hasty survey and decided with only two patrons nursing beers within that it was too early to hit the poker table.

The instant he stepped from the hotel a brisk northerly wind reminded him of the coat he had forgotten to retrieve from the cobbler yesterday afternoon. Rubbing his arms to fight off the cold, he picked his way across the muddy street. The bootsmith had the coat waiting on a rack by the door. As promised the rips were patched. Although the coat would never be termed high fashion, it did cut the wind. He didn't ask for anything more.

Following the cobbler's directions, Chance found a café and ordered a combination breakfast and lunch that consisted of a stack of wheatcakes, pork chops, and a mug of steaming black coffee. He was halfway through the small feast when John Tolbert settled in an empty chair across the table from him.

"Almost didn't recognize you, Sharpe." The deputy waved for a waitress to bring him a coffee and a piece of apple pie. "Haircut, shave, and bath, I'd say. Someone's going to mistake you for human, if you don't watch out."

The gambler ignored the lawman's attempt at humor. "Just availed myself of a few of Beltin's more civilized offerings last night."

Tolbert nodded while he took a bite of the pie and washed it down with a swig of coffee. "Expected to see you turn up at the jail last night and take Sheriff Pardee up on his offer of a free cot."

Before Chance could swallow, the deputy continued, "Went checking on you since I didn't want a guest in our town to go and freeze himself to death in the snow. Heard that you had some luck at cards last night."

"Some." The gambler offered no further information.

Tolbert smiled as he ate another bite of pie. "Charlie Lafare said you rented a room in his hotel. I went up to see how you were doing. When I knocked on the door, there was no answer. Got the same results about nine this morning."

"You seem to be taking an unusual interest in my welfare." Chance hid a growing irritation by wolfing down two quick mouthfuls of pork chop.

Tolbert shrugged. "Seems I've caused you more than your share of misery, Chance. Just trying to see that you stay in one piece until I can get you shipped out of town."

"Sharpe, remember?" the gambler corrected. He then cast a questioning glance at the lawman. "Any reason why I shouldn't remain in one piece?"

"Not really, but I didn't see any harm in heading off trouble before it started," Tolbert said as he finished his pie.

"What trouble?" Chance pressed, unable to contain his irritation any longer.

"Frank Clancy," the deputy replied. "He and the other boys came in late last night. Beltin's a small place. Sooner or later you're going to run head-on into those men. I don't want you tangling with them."

"Then tell them to stay clear of me." The gambler placed his fork on his plate and stared directly into Tolbert's eyes. "The way I see it, Clancy and his friends each owe me an apology—one way or the other."

"It's the *other* that's got me worried," the deputy said. "I've already laid it on the line to Frank and the boys, and I'll tell you the same thing. If there's any trouble, even so much as a raised voice, between you, I'll lock everyone of you in jail and throw away the key until the spring thaw. I barely stopped one mistake from happening; I don't want to count on my luck to stop another. Understand?"

"You definitely have a strange sense of hospitality here in the Dakota Territory." Chance returned to his meal.

Tolbert downed the last of his coffee, wiped his mouth with a red and white checkered napkin, tossed it to the table, and rose. "Forewarned is forearmed, Sharpe."

Chance nodded. "At least you're getting the name straight."

The deputy glared at him for a long, heavy moment, then pivoted and strode from the café. The gambler's gaze followed him through the café's windows as he stalked toward the jail. Chance smiled. Let Tolbert believe whatever he wanted, but tangling with five men was not part of the gambler's plan during his stay in Beltin. The odds were far too lopsided, especially for a man whose only weapon was a stiletto nestled in his boot.

On the other hand, should he happen to run into Clancy or one of his friends in a dark alley, he wouldn't be opposed to teaching them a lesson in common courtesy!

Chance stared at the miniature towers of chips before him on the table while the man beside him raked in a three-dollar pot. The gambler frowned. Thirty minutes ago the chips had tallied an even two hundred dollars—a hundred more than when he had begun the afternoon game. Now the stacks totaled one hundred ninety dollars.

Nickels and dimes, Chance tried to mentally write off the loss. He couldn't. In a game where the stakes *were* nickels and dimes, ten dollars was measured as financial disaster. Especially when those ten dollars had been taken by an underhanded dealer.

The gambler's steel blue eyes lifted from the white, red, and blue chips and shifted to the man on his left. Still damp from the falling snow outside, the clean-shaven man had taken a chair at the table an hour ago after introducing himself as Zeke Tatum. His announced intention was a few hours relaxation then a long night's sleep before riding north, where he had a job as an army scout waiting for him.

Chance had no way of verifying Tatum's story. What he did know about the man was that Tatum was a cheat—a sloppy one at that! The last two times Tatum dealt, the gambler had seen him palm cards.

Nickels and dimes, the thought repeated in Chance's mind. Caution told him to simply excuse himself from the table and avoid trouble. After all, Tatum had a .44 caliber Colt strapped to his hip, and all he had was a stiletto sheathed in his boot. There was no way to get to the blade without drawing attention. *Only a fool would accuse an armed man of cheating without a pistol to back up the accusation.*

It should have ended there, with Chance folding and surrendering his chair. However, there was also a matter of principal. Fair play was not a meaningless term to the gambler—it was a way of life! Chance Sharpe had never allowed a cheat to walk away from a gaming table with his ill-gotten gains stuffed in his pockets.

Nor do I intend to start now! From the corner of his eye Chance studied the man's pistol butt. Even with a left arm still stiff from injuries, he should be able to block Tatum's right hand when he went for the six-shooter. Then he'd have to rely on his own good right to take the fight out of the scout.

"Five card draw," Tatum announced as he began to deal. "Jacks or better to open, deuces wild."

Five times around the table Tatum went, counting aloud as he dealt. "There we go, five cards for everybody."

"I count five for everybody—except you," Chance said as the man reached for his cards.

Tatum's head twisted toward the gambler. "What? What are you getting at?"

"You've three extra cards in the palm of your left hand—royality I'd wager. I saw you slip them from the bottom of the deck." Chance met the man's glaring brown eyes but kept a close watch on his right hand at the periphery of his vision.

The other four players at the table abruptly pushed away, fear paling their faces.

"You calling me a cheat, farmer?" Tatum demanded, his eyes narrowing to slits.

"That's exactly what I'm—"

Chance didn't have the opportunity to finish his sentence. Tatum's right hand went for the Colt. The instant the gambler saw the movement, his left arm slashed out.

His balled fist hammered solidly atop Tatum's wrist, slamming his hand away from the revolver.

Simultaneously, Chance shoved from his chair. His right arm lashed out to drive a fist directly into Tatum's face.

With a surprise grunt the still seated scout tumbled backward to spill onto the floor. Again his right hand went for the Colt holstered on his hip.

"I wouldn't even think about it." The double click of a cocking hammer punctuated the words of Deputy John Tolbert, who stepped from the bar with his own pistol leveled at the man on the floor. Tatum's hand jerked away from the Colt's butt. Tolbert tilted his head at Chance. "Sharpe, get his gun and hand it to me."

The gambler did just that. "I didn't notice you at the bar. Keeping an eye on me?"

"Thought Frank Clancy might pay the Golden Eagle a visit," Tolbert said as he broke open the pistol and emptied its loads onto the floor. "How much did he take you for?"

"Me—ten dollars. He also skinned the others," Chance replied. "He sat down at the table with twenty-five dollars."

The lawman glanced to Charles Lafare, who had been among the players. "Charlie, cash in his chips. Give Sharpe here his ten and let me have this polecat's original twenty-five. Divide the rest between the boys."

The hotel and saloon owner raked Tatum's chips from the table. A few minutes later he handed Chance a ten-dollar gold piece and passed twenty-five in bills to the deputy. Tolbert bent down and stuffed fifteen bills into Tatum's coat pocket. "You've just been fined ten dollars for creating a public nuisance."

The lawman tossed the empty Colt atop the scout's belly. "You've got exactly ten seconds to get your ass out that door, mount, and ride from town. One . . . two . . ."

Tatum scrambled to his feet without bothering to gather the spilled loads from the floor around him. On Tolbert's five count he pushed through the Golden Eagle's double doors at a dead run. By nine he was spurring his mount northward.

Without another word, the deputy holstered his pistol and walked from the saloon.

Close, Chance thought as he returned to the table to collect his chips. Excusing himself from the game, he walked to the cage and exchanged the wooden pieces of red, white, and blue for cash. He then exited the saloon. There was a .44 caliber Remington in a glass case inside the general store that he should have purchased the moment he had awakened that morning.

TWELVE

Chance studied Marilee while she sat across the café table from him. Her own gaze was riveted to the falling snow outside the window. The powderlike flurries had given way to big wet flakes as the grayness of the overcast day faded to night. No longer was the snow melting when it hit the ground. All of Beltin paled with the snowy cover.

"Still thinking about California?" the gambler asked.

Marilee's head turned from the window, and she smiled weakly at him. "Wondering how anything that has disappointed me as much as this snow can be so beautiful. I really do enjoy the snow. I never saw that much of it as a child. When it gets cold in New Orleans, it rains."

"When it gets hot in New Orleans, it rains." Chance grinned, recalling the old delta joke that the Crescent City had but one rainy season that began on January 1 and ended December 31.

"It is beautiful, isn't it?" The young singer gave the snow one last glance before returning to their simple evening meal of chicken and dumplings.

"Yes," the gambler answered, trying not to consider the fact that a heavy snow could very well maroon him in Beltin for longer than he cared to think about.

His gaze moved back to Marilee. Actually the situation wouldn't be that bad. He couldn't think of a more lovely—or lively—companion with which to spend a cold winter.

"You're gathering a few stares, Chance." Marilee interrupted his musings with an impish smile. Her emerald eyes darted to the side, indicating the café's other male customers.

"I noticed that the moment we entered," he replied. "Although, I think *glares* come closer to the truth."

"Beltin's not used to seeing me with a man," Marilee explained.

"I thought that I detected a hint of jealousy hanging in the air." The gambler remembered Doc Henry's comment last night about the majority of the townsmen's willingness to give an arm to be with the blond. It was easy enough to understand the glares. He *was* a stranger who had just ridden into town and snatched a prize, coveted by Beltin's male population, right out from under their noses.

"It's getting late." Marilee placed her spoon on her plate. "I should return to the hotel. I go on at eight o'clock, and it takes me about an hour to dress."

Chance nodded and hastily spooned down the last two bites of his chicken and dumplings. He had pushed from his chair and held Marilee's coat open for her by the time she rose. He felt every male eye in the café follow them outside, each of their owners silently wishing that he could exchange places with the gambler.

"Burrrr!" Marilee shivered aloud, her breath coming from her lips in a white mist. She hugged her coat closer and hastened her strides. "There's something that I'd forgotten about snow—it's *cold!*"

"The thorn of winter's white rose." Chance laughed while he quickened his own pace to keep up with her.

That thorn had quite a nip, the gambler admitted when white flakes struck his cheek and clung there, stinging like cold needles as they melted. For a second time that evening the snow thrust his eastward journey to the forefront of his thoughts. Winter travel was bad at its best; snow only increased the difficulty.

Not that I'm that close to leaving Beltin, he told himself. While he had purchased the .44 caliber Remington now slung from a holster on his hip, he remained short of the 175 dollars Harrison Clive, Beltin's blacksmith and livery stable owner, wanted for a horse, saddle, and pack mule. Once those were his, he still faced the problem of raising the money for a rifle and supplies.

After a quick mental tally, the gambler realized three hundred dollars should cover his needs and give him a small stake for paddlewheeler fare once he reached the Missouri River. Three hundred dollars—a kingly sum, especially if he expected to win it at nickel and dime games! He glanced at Marilee; her thousand dollars was more than three times distance than the sum he needed.

Abruptly the singer's quick strides stopped. A puzzled frown darkened the delicate features of her oval face. Her head cocked from side to side. "Do you hear anything?"

Chance listened and was about to answer no when he detected the rumble of horses—a lot of them!

"Get back!" Marilee grasped his right arm and tugged him into the shadow of an alley separating two wooden buildings.

"Wha—" Chance attempted to protest. His momentary surprise was forgotten.

Seven riders, each with rifle in hand, reined their mounts down Beltin's Main Street. Dirt and snow flew from the animals' hooves in a mucky shower. However, it wasn't the dirt that Marilee and a dozen of Beltin's other residents sank back to avoid.

"Who are they?" The gambler stepped from the alley.

Five buildings from his position, the riders jerked their mounts to a halt in front of the jail. The men were rough-looking, cloaked in heavy coats of deer and bear hide that marked them as trappers rather than farmers—as did the heavy bore of the Sharps rifles they carried.

"Chance, get back here," Marilee reached for his arm again. She moaned in frustration when he brushed her away. "There'll be trouble. It's none of our business."

"Who are they?" Chance repeated, unable to make out the riders' features in the dim yellow glow that escaped the jail's single window.

"It's the Ransons!" Marilee found his arm on her second try, but the gambler refused to budge. "Old man Clay's come after his son. There will be trouble!"

Chance pried her clenching fingers from his arm. Mumbling under her breath, Marilee gave up and moved back into the alley's concealing darkness. "If you get shot, don't blame me."

The gambler didn't listen to her. His ears homed to a rider who edged his horse directly toward the jail's entrance.

"Glen, Glen Pardee," the man called out. "This here's Clay Ranson. You got my youngest in there. I've come to fetch him."

The window's light washed across the face of the patriarch of the Ranson clan. Grizzled and weather-beaten, Clay Ranson's features were like tanned leather that had wrinkled and cracked with time. Dark stubble, sprinkled with a scattering of white, shadowed his cheeks and chin as he scowled at the jail's door, which remained unopened.

"Pardee!" Ranson's voice rose two angry levels when he shouted again. "I ain't a man who takes kindly to being made to wait. Pardee, you come out here!"

The gambler's gaze shifted to the six mounted men behind Clay Ranson. His sons, Chance realized, recalling John Tolbert's mentioning that Ranson had seven sons. The seventh was now locked behind bars for robbery and murder. The window's glow was too dim for him to judge their ages and features.

"Pardee, you don't want to rile me," the head of Ranson clan continued to shout. "If you make me step down and walk . . ."

The door to the jail opened. Silhouetted by the interior light Sheriff Glen Pardee stepped across the threshold to face the father and sons. He held a rifle in his arms as did Deputy John Tolbert, who Chance could barely glimpse standing in the doorway.

"I'm here, Clay," the sheriff calmly answered Ranson. "What can I do for you?"

"We've come for Martin," Ranson answered. "Bring him out to us, and we'll ride away all quiet like."

Pardee paused, then sucked at his teeth. "I reckon you can see how I can't do that, Clay. Martin up and robbed the bank. Shot Wes Clancy when he tried to stop him."

"I want my boy, Sheriff," Ranson answered.

"You'll have to stand in line," Pardee said. "A marshal on his way from Fargo has first rights to him. Then a U.S. judge and jury has their say."

"Ain't no need for no marshal, judge, or jury," Ranson replied without pause. "Anybody in town see Martin rob the bank and shoot that teller?"

Again Pardee paused as though carefully choosing his words. "There weren't no eyeball witnesses, Clay. But there ain't no need for them. I picked up Martin's tracks outside the bank. Found 'em again on the edge of town and followed 'em. Caught up with your son at the Rocky Run of Potter's Creek. He still had the empty bank money bags in his saddlebags."

"Empty money bags don't prove nothing," Clay Ranson said with a shake of his head.

"That marshal in Fargo and I think different," Pardee answered. "Anyway, the matter's up to a judge and jury to decide. It's getting us nowhere standing here talking in the cold."

Ranson's head slowly turned from side to side as though he tried to glance at his six sons who sat mounted behind him. When he looked back to the sheriff, he said, "Then you ain't going to give Martin to me and my boys?"

"I'm afraid that I can't, Clay," Pardee answered with a shake of his head. "Reckon you can see how it is."

"Yes." Ranson's tone grew low and cold. "And I reckon you understand how I can't let no marshal go draggin' my flesh and blood off to Fargo."

Without warning, Ranson's rifle swung up. A blue-and-yellow blossom of fire spat from its muzzle. The thunder of exploding black powder shattered the night. A single slug of lead hammered into Sheriff Pardee's chest. The impact lifted him from his feet and threw him back through the doorway and into Tolbert. The two lawmen spilled to the floor of the jail.

"Let your guns do our talking!" Clay Ranson reined his horse back out of the line of fire.

Six rifles leaped up. From the corner of an eye Chance saw the jail door slam shut. Then those six rifles spoke, each blasting into the wooden structure. The single-shot weapons empty, the seven Ransons freed pistols and began firing into the jail. The building's single window exploded in a shower of silvery fragments; splinters of wood rained through the air.

And then silence filled Beltin.

"Deputy!" Clay Ranson shouted. "That's just a sample of what we've got in mind for you, if'n you ain't got more sense than your boss. Me and my boys'll be back for Martin tomorrow night. Make sure he's waiting for us, or we'll burn this whole damned town down. You understand me?"

Two shots from inside the jail barked in answer. The Ransons ducked. There was no need; the shots went wild, missing all seven riders.

"Tomorrow night," Clay Ranson shouted again. "It's either Martin or you!"

With that, Ranson wheeled his mount about and spurred it northward. His sons drove their horses on at his heels.

Behind them, the jail's door flew open. John Tolbert ran into the street to cry, "Stop them! Dammit! Stop them, they've shot Sheriff Pardee!" The deputy's pistol rose, and he fired after the retreating men.

Chance reacted to Tolbert's plea for aid rather than thinking. The Remington had half cleared its holster when Marilee jumped from the alley.

"No!" With both hands she grabbed the gambler's right arm and pulled with all her might.

The six-shooter fell from Chance's hand, discharging when it struck the ground. Off balance, the gambler's footing slipped in the wet snow. Together Marilee and he tumbled into the cold wetness.

"Somebody over thataway took a shot at us!" one of the Ransons shouted.

Seven pistols answered the bark of Chance's fallen weapon. Hot lead whined above the prone man and woman. Then there was only the sound of retreating hooves.

Heaving a sigh of disgust, the gambler pushed to his feet to help Marilee from the ground. The cold glare freezing his features were enough to pale the singer's face.

"I had to stop you, Chance," Marilee pleaded. "I lost you once, I wasn't going to let it happen again! The Ransons would have cut you down."

The concern in her eyes and tone cooled the simmering rage in his breast. Before he could raise his arms and draw her close, John Tolbert called, "Help! Somebody help me! Sheriff Pardee's been shot. Someone get Doc Henry!"

Chance glanced at the blond singer. "Go to the hotel. I'll meet you in the Golden Eagle later."

With that he ran from the alley to aid the deputy.

* * *

Tolbert chewed at the cigar Chance had given him rather than smoking it. The deputy sat slump-shouldered in Doc Henry's parlor, his eyes occasionally lifting to a dark-stained wooden door behind which the physician worked to save Glen Pardee's life.

Finding no words to comfort the lawman, the gambler kept his silence and watched the falling snow outside. A white blanket four inches deep now covered Beltin's streets.

"Son of a bitch!" Tolbert slammed a fist into the padded arm of his chair. "That bastard Ranson didn't even give us a hint of what he had in mind. He'd cut Glen down before I knew what he intended."

"The sheriff knew what he was facing when he stepped outside," Chance offered. "The shooting wasn't your fault."

His words didn't help. The deputy ground the cigar between his teeth. "I should have known better than to trust that old bastard. You can see the mean streak in him from a mile away! It's the same with his sons. I should have known!"

Before the gambler could answer, the dark-stained door opened. Doc Henry stepped out, looked at Tolbert, and heaved a weary sigh.

"He didn't make it, did he, Doc?" The deputy slowly rose from the chair. "Glen's dead, isn't he?"

The physician nodded. "I did what I could, John, but it wasn't enough. The bullet was too close to his heart. He never had a chance."

Tolbert's face went as hard as granite when his eyes lifted to the door concealing the body of his dead friend.

"If it will help, John, I'll get Wade Glevis and make the funeral arrangements," Doc Henry said. "The town will handle the costs. It owes Glen that much."

The deputy said nothing and continued to glare at the closed door.

"You need to get some rest tonight, John. You've been through a lot." Doc Henry reached into a pocket to produce a blue-tinted bottle. "Mix a spoonful of this with some water and drink it. It'll taste a mite bitter, but it'll help you sleep."

"It's not sleep I want." Tolbert's voice was strained and tight. "It's not sleep I want."

"John, I don't know what foolish notions you've got in your head, but you'd best put them aside," Doc Henry said. "Beltin's lost one good man tonight. We can't afford to lose another."

Without a word or a nod of acknowledgment, Tolbert pivoted, walked to the doctor's front door, and threw it open.

"Tolbert," Chance called after the deputy when he stepped outside. "Tolbert, what are you going to do?"

The lawman didn't answer, but kept walking into the falling snow.

THIRTEEN

Chance eased from beneath the covers and stepped to the cold wooden floor. Behind him Marilee moaned, "There's no reason to leave. It's warmer in here."

"The thought of spending the day bundled in the bed sheets with you is quite attractive, but . . ." The gambler shrugged while he moved to the hearth to stoke another log atop the cherry-glowing embers.

"But Lady Luck calls you." The blond singer sat up in the bed, pillows fluffed behind her back and covers clutched about her. A little pout tugged down the corners of her mouth. "I would think you'd find my charms more attractive than a poker table."

"I do, but a man doesn't live on charms alone." He grinned then artfully ducked a pillow Marilee sent sailing at his head. After assuring that the singer didn't intend another missile in retaliation for his remark, he scooped his pants from the floor and stepped into them.

"It looks like it's still snowing outside." Marilee pulled the bed covers high, tucking them beneath her chin. "No wonder it's so cold."

The gambler moved beside the window and glanced out. The heavy snow that had begun last night still fell. A white blanket at least a foot deep covered Beltin's streets and clung to the roofs of the town's buildings. "It doesn't appear to be letting up any."

"Terrific!" Marilee snorted. "It looks like Beltin will be my home until the spring thaw."

"There's always the southern route to California," Chance suggested while he surveyed the street below. "You could head into Texas and find someone traveling across the New Mexico and Arizona Territories. Or you might sail around the cape. It's summer below the equator."

"It takes money for both of those routes," Marilee replied. "Something we're both short of at the moment."

Which was the very reason Chance had forced himself from the seductive luxury of Marilee's bed. Townsmen seeking to try their luck at the deal of cards would soon come wandering into the Golden Eagle Saloon—if the heavy snow didn't keep them away. *On the other hand the snow might bring them in,* he thought. A saloon was an excellent place to escape being trapped at home with a nagging wife and screaming children.

The gambler's thoughts of the Golden Eagle were momentarily forgotten. He recognized John Tolbert outside. The deputy exited a seed and feed store and entered a barbershop right next door.

"How did the cards go for you last night?" Marilee asked. "After the shooting, things seemed to be a bit slow."

"Well enough," Chance answered absent-mindedly. Tolbert re-emerged from the barber's and walked into the cobbler's shop beside it.

"It sounds like you're starting to build up a bankroll," the singer continued. "I'd be careful, if I were you. In a town this low on hard cash someone might decide to roll you."

"The thought had occurred to me. Any suggestions? I don't think Beltin's bank is exactly what you could call a safe depository." The gambler watched the lawman step from the cobbler's and move into the funeral home.

"I keep mine in an envelope tacked behind the dresser mirror. Hide yours there if you like," the singer answered.

"I might just do that." Chance followed Tolbert's shop-by-shop journey from the undertaker's into the land office.

"What's so interesting out there?"

"John Tolbert," the gambler replied, explaining the man's actions. "Wonder what he's up to?"

"I don't know or care," Marilee answered. "Probably has something to do with the Ransons, if I had to take a guess."

"Probably," Chance agreed when he turned from the window and pulled on his shirt. "You know anything about Clay Ranson and his tribe?"

The blond shook her head. "Never met any of them, except for Martin."

"The one locked in the jail?"

"The same," she said. "I've talked to him a few times in the Golden Eagle. I think that he was a little infatuated with me."

"I bet he was," Chance chuckled, silently wondering if Marilee encouraged that infatuation. And knowing damned well that in all likelihood she had.

"Martin used to talk a lot about running away to San Francisco and taking me with him," the singer went on. "But that's all it was—talk. He had no more money than I did."

Chance took half of his two hundred dollars and placed it in the envelope tacked behind the dresser mirror. He'd find a safer place for the money later, but for now the envelope beat carrying around a wad of bills that might attract greedy eyes.

He turned back to Marilee and said, "I wouldn't call it all talk. It's apparent that Martin had a good idea where to get the money he wanted."

Marilee shrugged. "A lot of good it did him. He'll end up hanging, if his pa doesn't manage to get him killed trying to break him out of jail."

"Guess you're right there." Chance walked to the bed and kissed her lips. "Meet me down in the Golden Eagle when you're ready to eat."

"It'll be hours," Marilee answered with an impish glint in her emerald eyes. "Somebody kept me up most of the night."

Chance grinned as he walked to the room's door. "The same could be said of me."

Another hurled pillow thudded against the wood as he closed the door behind him.

Chance sipped idly at a beer that had lost its head a half hour ago. Except for the bartender, the piano player, and himself, the Golden Eagle was empty, exactly the way it had been when he entered two hours earlier. The gambler glanced to the saloon's windows; although it had lightened, snow still feel outside.

"They'll be coming in soon," the bartender said, apparently noticing his only customer's gaze. "Soon as the men start feeling penned up in their homes, they'll come trugging in. That's the way it always is. Tonight will be as busy as a Saturday night, unless I miss my bet."

"I'll drink to that." Chance lifted his mug to the bartender and slipped at the flat brew.

A frigid blast of air sliced through the saloon as the double doors flew open. John Tolbert strode in, snow caked to his clothing. His dark eyes narrowed as he surveyed the empty saloon. Like a man carrying the world on his shoulders, he walked to the end of the bar and waved the bartender to him. In tones too low for Chance to discern, the two men talked for several minutes. Eventually the bartender shook his head and stepped away from the lawman, "It's not my job, John. I've got a wife and two sons to think about."

The deputy's gaze went to the piano; the musician who had toyed at the ivory keys all afternoon was nowhere to be found. Tolbert's eyes, heavy with worry, shifted to Chance and hung on the gambler an instant before the deputy turned and wearily trod back outside.

"What was that all about?" Chance's right eyebrow arched.

"A crazy man," the bartender answered, "that's what that was about. The deputy's been out all day, trying to round up men for tonight."

"To go against the Ransons?" Chance watched Tolbert cross the street to the jail.

"He thinks the men in this town are as loco as he is." The bartender shook his head in disbelief. "Everyone in town heard Clay Ranson threaten to burn Beltin to the ground last night. The old man will do it, too, if any of us go up against him. Ain't no man in Beltin that mad, except maybe Frank Clancy. He might join up with Tolbert. Of course, he's got a reason. It was Martin Ranson that killed his brother Wesley."

"The Ransons are that bad?" The gambler saw Tolbert disappear inside the jail. He felt a twinge of guilt, but only a twinge. Clay Ranson and his sons weren't his problem. He wouldn't have ever heard of this town if Tolbert hadn't mistakenly arrested him and dragged him across the Dakota Territory.

"Bad don't halfway describe the Ransons," the bartender answered. "The sons are mean as alley mongrels. Ain't a Saturday night that goes by without one of them getting into a fight for the pleasure of busting up another man's face. Their daddy's a hundred times worse. 'Fore we got law here in Beltin, I once seen Clay Ranson carve up a man with a hunting knife just because the fellar accidently spilled a drink on his coat sleeve. Ain't nobody want to be on that man's wrong side—if he's got a good side to start with!"

"But there's only seven of them," Chance said. "Surely a whole town can stand against seven men?"

"If it was only Clay and his boys a man had to fret about, I reckon you'd be right," the bartender answered. "But this whole country's stinking with Ransons. Clay's got kin scattered near and far through the Territory. One word from that old bastard and he can call in a small army to ride with him. Like as not, he'll have his kinfolk with him when he comes back tonight."

The bartender paused and glanced toward the jail. "No, sir, ain't no man in this town crazy enough to match guns with the Ransons—no man except John Tolbert. And all he'll get is himself killed for the effort."

Chance took another sip from the beer. He knew what he'd do if he were wearing the deputy's boots. If Beltin's citizens didn't care enough to fight for their town, then there was no need for a man sticking out his own neck for such people. However, he wasn't standing in Tolbert's boots, and he had the feeling the lawman had no intention of turning Martin Ranson over to his father tonight.

"Four sevens"—Chance spread his hand atop the green felt covering the table—"and an ace."

"Beats me!" Doc Henry tossed down his cards and stared sourly at three kings.

In turn, the five other players admitted defeat while they threw in their hands. Chance's arms reached out and raked in the small mountain of chips at the center of the table. His mental calculations brought his total bankroll to three hundred dollars. "Gentlemen, it has been both a pleasurable and profitable evening. I think the time has come for me to call it a night."

"Thank God," Harrison Clive said with a sigh of obvious relief. "If you'd won another hand, I'd've upped the price on that gelding and mule I quoted you yesterday by another twenty-five dollars just to get back a piece of what you've gotten from me."

"Maybe my luck will change for the better now," the saloon's proprietor, Charles Lafare, said as he gathered in the cards and began to shuffle. "Anybody waiting for that chair, or is it going to go vacant?"

A man in a stained brown hat and bear-fur coat sank into the seat the gambler abandoned. The man glanced at Chance. "Hope you left some of your luck in this chair. I could use a tad."

Arms weighted by their burden of colored chips, the gambler crossed the saloon to the cage and dumped them into the teller's lap. "Two hundred dollars even, according to my count."

While the teller busied himself sorting and counting, Chance glanced about the saloon. The bartender's earlier prediction had proven true. In spite of the snow and the Ransons' threat to return to town that night, the Golden Eagle was packed from wall to wall. And the townsmen had suddenly found a well spring of wealth. Each seemed to have more than enough money to sample the saloon's spirits as well as try their hand at the various games of chance.

Money tucked away in socks and mattresses for just such an occasion, Chance thought with a tug of regret in his breast for abandoning the poker table so early in the night.

Mustn't get greedy, he reprimanded himself. He had set a goal of three hundred dollars—the money needed for a horse and supplies to get him back to the Missouri River—and reached it. Only a fool would risk a sudden swing in luck that might cost him all he had won. Chance Sharpe was no fool.

"Mr. Sharpe," the teller spoke up, "you made a mistake in counting your chips."

The gambler pivoted and stared at the man, ready for the worst.

"Your total came to two hundred and ten dollars." The teller pushed a stack of bills through the cage's window.

Tension flowed from Chance's body, and he smiled. "Ten dollars extra to do a little celebrating on."

Carefully depositing the wad of bills deep in his pants pocket, Chance wove his way through the saloon's crowd to find a place at the bar. "Two fingers of Kentucky bourbon," he called to the bartender.

The man immediately responded by sliding a glass aslosh with amber liquor toward the gambler. A hush fell over the saloon as Chance lifted the drink toward his lips. Glancing into the mirror behind the bar, he saw the reason for the abrupt silence. John Tolbert stood in the doorway.

"Sorry to disturb you good citizens of Beltin,"—the deputy made no attempt to disguise the contempt in his voice,—"just making my nightly rounds. None of us wants any trouble in town, do we?"

Although every eye in the Golden Eagle was riveted to the lawman, not one man spoke, even in greeting. A sad little smile played at the corners of Tolbert's lips. Chance shook his head; maybe the bartender had been right—the deputy was crazy. He was a defeated man and too stubborn to admit it. To top that, not one of Beltin's brave citizens gave a damn.

In a silent toast to Tolbert's insanity, the gambler once again lifted his glass toward the deputy's reflection in the mirror. The bourbon never touched Chance's lips. There at the entrance to the hotel, three men edged into the Golden Eagle. An icy finger traced up the gambler's spine. Although he had never seen their faces before, there was no mistaking the men's features—Clay Ranson's sons. And all were going for the six-shooters on their hips!

"Tolbert! The hotel door!" Chance refused to allow a man who had saved his life to be gunned down without warning. "Three Ransons!"

The gambler spun. His right hand dropped to his waist and found the butt of his Remington. The Golden Eagle's patrons, sensing impending gunplay, dropped to the floor to escape being caught in the line of fire. Across the room one of the Ransons swung to face Chance.

By the time the Remington's barrel freed leather, Chance's thumb had tugged the hammer back. His right arm swung upward, and he pointed rather than aimed the pistol's muzzle while his trigger finger squeezed inward.

Thunder exploded through the saloon. Clouds of dark smoke billowed from the gambler's revolver while he fired off three shots as rapidly as he could cock and pull the trigger. He was vaguely aware of other barking guns and the waspish buzz of hot lead in the air. However, he was more aware of the fact that no burning brands of death tore into his body.

Then there was silence.

The blinding cloud of smoke parted. The three Ransons lay crumpled on the saloon's floor, blood flowing from their bodies to mingle with the dirt. Chance's head slowly turned. John Tolbert still stood, smoking Colt in his hand. Whether it was the Colt or the Remington that had cut the men down didn't matter. They both still lived.

"Drag their bodies outside and pile them in front of the jail," the deputy ordered as he holstered his pistol. "If Clay Ranson shows up tonight, he'll know where he can find them."

Ten of the saloon's patrons scrambled to carry out the lawman's command. Chance smiled grimly. *Too bad they aren't as eager to defend their own town.*

While the three bodies were dragged out into the snow, Tolbert crossed to the gambler's side. "You surprise me, Chance. I didn't see you as one taking a side in this. I don't know what made you change your mind and decide to join me, but I'm damned glad about it."

Chance held up his hands and waved the lawman off. "You're taking a lot for granted, Deputy. I haven't chosen any sides nor have I thrown in with you. I saw three men about to gun down one. All I did was even the odds a bit. Your fight with the Ransons isn't mine."

Tolbert's eyes narrowed as he glared at the gambler. Then his head moved from side to side. "I hope you're right, but whether you like it or not you might have just made a choice. Those are Ransons lying out there by the jail—and Ransons don't take kindly to anyone who goes around killing their kin."

The deputy turned and walked outside without a glance back at the gambler. Chance watched him leave. Tolbert was wrong; the fight wasn't his. He had his three hundred dollars, and by this time tomorrow night Beltin would be just a bad memory.

FOURTEEN

Chance awoke to the soft insistence of Marilee's lips. His eyes opened to roll down to the source of warm pleasure that suffused his body. The frosty mist of the singer's blond hair bobbed while the moist cradle of her mouth brought him to life.

A deep sigh working from his throat, he lifted his hands to caress the sides of her face. Beneath his stroking fingertips he felt her cheeks hollow and fill with each dipping motion of her head. He controlled the surging needs that mounted within him and forced his body to remain motionless while he savored the laving swirls of Marilee's tongue.

She taunted and teased until his quivering muscles began to move on their own volition. Then her lips slid from him. Her head tilted up. A hungry emerald fire burned at the core of her eyes as a satisfied smile moved across her lips.

Chance's palms cupped her face. "You have a delightful way of rousing a man in the morning."

"*A*-rousing," she corrected while her hand crept upward to glide over his naked chest. "You mentioned wanting to be up early this morning."

The gambler grinned. He had wanted to arise early, but his intentions had obviously been quite different than those of this marvelous woman. With three hundred dollars safely tucked away in the envelope behind Marilee's mirror, he had planned a quick call on Beltin's livery stable and general store for a mount and supplies, then beginning his long journey eastward.

However, he thought as he soaked in Marilee's supple body, *those plans aren't chiseled in stone!*

Moving from her cheeks, his hands moved across her bare shoulders. She moaned as excited waves of gooseflesh ripples over her body. Downward his fingers traced, pausing long enough to bring the dark, fleshy cherries topping the creamy mounds of her breasts to attention and a series of soft, wanton groans from her throat. When his hands slid downward once again, it was to take her slender waist and draw her into the bed beside him.

Again, Marilee's and his intentions were quite different. Before his palms reached their destination, the blond's own hands gently pushed his aside. That hungry blaze still aflame in her gem-hued eyes, she moved forward on all fours like some feline predator stalking its prey.

While Chance lay flat on his back, mesmerized by the singer's beauty, she straddled his hips. With a hand firmly clapsed about him, she rose on her knees to slowly descend, guiding him into the heated harbor of her body. The moans that trembled over her lips mingled with his in a chorus of desire.

Again her hands returned to his chest; this time to brace herself as her pelvis began a tantalizing, undulating slow-motion dance. Her head thrust back, and her breath came in a short, quick rhythm. Her eyes—now containing that drunken gaze of pleasure—closed as she lost herself in her own carnal needs.

Once more the gambler forced his hips to remain motionless, allowing this delightful bundle of woman to ride him. While her pelvis gyrated about him in grasping swirls of growing passion, his palms rose to capture the elongated cones of flesh that dangled so temptingly from her chest.

She offered no protest to the expert ministrations of his knowing hands. Instead, her body responded in a tempo of urgency. She rocked atop him; her breaths were sharp pants of nearing release.

Only then did his body move, easily falling into the demanding rhythm of her hips. A cry of pleasure achieved tore from her lips. Her outstretched arms quivered, then quaked, then gave way beneath her. Chance drew her close, holding her tightly as his own release surged forth.

Her limp body atop his, they lay there until the last trembly spasm of lust quieted. When she rolled from him, it was to nestle her head in the hollow of his shoulder. Neither spoke, but simply allowed their stroking palms to caress the reality of each other's body.

Chance wasn't certain how long they lay there. However, the tug of daylight outside eventually drew his head toward the hotel room's windows. Above Beltin's snow-covered rooftops he saw a cloudless blue sky. He couldn't have asked for a better day to begin his ride back to the Missouri River.

"When are you leaving?"

Marilee's voice startled him; his head twisted around to discover the blond's gaze on the window. Her emerald eyes shifted to him. "When are you leaving?"

"You knew?"

Marilee's head lifted from his shoulder as she propped on an elbow. "I saw you placing two hundred in the envelope last night. That makes a total of three—exactly what you said you needed to get back to the river."

The gambler nodded while he slid his legs from beneath the covers and perched on the edge of the bed. "I still have to buy a mount and pack mule then purchase supplies before I head out."

She said nothing when he stood and began to dress. A chill that had nothing to do with the wintry weather outside crept into the room. Chance had hoped to avoid this, and would have if he had awakened before the singer.

"You were going to leave without telling me, weren't you?" Marilee's gaze remained on him.

"It had crossed my mind. A note with a wish that we might meet again under more favorable circumstances would have been easier," he admitted.

"Chance, that's not fair." She flung herself to her back and stared at the ceiling. "You're hitting below the belt. Things have changed between us."

"That's why I decided against the note." He tugged on his boots and walked back to the bed to sit on its edge once more. He took Marilee's hand in his own and lifted it to his lips. "After I bought the horse and supplies, I was going to come back."

"A quick good-bye to soothe your conscious?" Tears welled in her eyes and a quaver crept into her voice.

"My conscious doesn't need soothing. We're both all grown up now and knew exactly what we had gotten ourselves into." Chance shook his head, unwilling to accept the burden of guilt she tried to place on his shoulders. "I was going to try to convince you one more time to come with me."

"Don't lie, Chance." She wiped away the moisture that trickled down her cheeks. "There been no lies between us this time. Let's keep it that way."

"It's no lie. I want you to come with me—back to the Mississippi and the *Wild Card*," he said.

"Chance, you know that I—"

"Shhh," he hushed her. "I think that you can. There were no charges filed against you. And if the authorities decide to fabricate something, I have a good attorney that can handle whatever they trump up."

"But"—she stared at him, her head moving from side to side in doubt—"Chance I just ca—"

He placed a fingertip to her lips to silence her once again. Then he leaned forward and kissed those trembling lips.

"I don't want an answer now," he said when they parted. "I want you to take your time and consider the situation from all the angles. When I get back to the civilized world, I'll wire you a thousand dollars. You can make up your mind then. Use the money to return to New Orleans—or use it to get to California."

"Do you mean that?" A hint of disbelief still colored her expression.

Chance stood and gazed down at her. "No lies, Marilee. I want you to return to New Orleans, but the choice has to be yours. I won't force you into anything."

She offered no reply and sat in the bed biting at her lower lip.

Drawing a deep breath, the gambler crossed the room and lifted his coat from the back of a chair. After slipping into it and buttoning its front, he reached into the envelope behind the mirror and extracted his three hundred dollars. The wad of bills secure at the bottom of a coat pocket, he moved to the room's door and opened it. "Good-bye, Marilee."

She said nothing, nor did her eyes lift to him. Turning, he stepped over the threshold.

"Chance!" Marilee's voice brought his head around. "Chance, I love you."

It was his turn to find no words for a reply. He merely nodded, stepped from the room, and closed the door behind him.

Love. He wanted to believe her but refused to consider the possibility as he descended the wooden stairs to the hotel's lobby. Marilee had uttered a promise of love once before, and he had believed it. This time he wasn't so eager to offer his own heart.

When he reached the river, he would wire the singer the thousand dollars he had promised. She could make her choice then. If she came to New Orleans, then would come his time of choosing. Until then . . .

The gambler shoved away the "ifs" crowding his head. There were too many of them to attempt to second-guess the future. What would be, would be. And he would live with it. There was nothing else to do.

A brief stop at the hotel's desk to pay his bill and Chance stepped outside into the bright Dakota morning. He shook his head and smiled. In spite of all the life it had displayed last night, Beltin looked like a ghost town this morning. Not one man or woman walked the snow-covered streets.

All hiding from the cold in their homes like rabbits crouched in holes for warmth. He reached into his pocket and squeezed the roll of bills. Let the people of Beltin hide from the weather; he welcomed it. Today would be his last day here on the edge of nowhere!

A stiff wind cut through his clothing as he started down Main Street. *Well, maybe not welcome it,* he admitted with a shiver, but he'd live with the cold as long as he was headed eastward. He added a pair of longjohns to the mental list of supplies to be purchased at the general store. *And a warm hat!*

The bark of a rifle shattered the gambler's reflections. A wet, sucking sound and a spray of snow erupted from the street a stride from his feet!

Chance's right hand freed the Remington from its holster while his head jerked from side to side. To his left—on the roof of a seamstress shop—two men crouched with rifles. *Ransons!* He had forgotten about the father and sons, but it was more than apparent that he had never left their minds.

While realization of his vulnerable position penetrated the gambler's brain, one of the men shouldered his rifle as the other began to reload. Chance leaped to the right, rather than wasting a wild shot. He hit the snow rolling. Behind him the second rifleman's bullet tore into the ground where he had stood but a heartbeat before.

His mind focused on hot lead rather than the cold snow that caked his clothing, Chance somersaulted to his feet in a crouch. The Remington whipped upward. He took a bead on the first gunman; his forefinger began to squeeze the pistol's trigger.

The gambler never completed the action!

A third rifle cracked and spat lead. An angry buzz whined by his right ear so close that he felt its heat as it sliced through the air.

Chance spun about. Two more riflemen knelt atop the roof of the barbershop on the opposite side of the street. Four men in all—and they had him neatly trapped between them in a deadly crossfire! He now understood why Beltin's streets were empty. The town had already displayed its unwillingness to make a stand against the Ranson clan.

Caught in the open, the gambler realized what an easy target he made. He refused to be a stationary one! Spinning about, he darted toward the north side of the street intent on crashing through the door to the seamstress shop. Once inside, out of those rifle sights, he would decide his next move.

His legs carried him two strides before two shots ripped into the snow in front of him. Chance's boot heels dug into the white blanket; he skidded to a wobbly halt, reversed his course and sprinted toward the other side of Main Street. A watering trough outside the seed and feed store offered partial shelter from the deadly hail of rifle bullets.

Again his legs carried him forward two quick strides. This time he anticipated the shots that would come. Throwing himself to the right, he plowed into the snow. Two rifles cracked from the rooftops; two slugs of lead dug harmlessly into the ground.

Scrambling to his feet, Chance once more ran. Rather than following a straight line to the trough, he zigged and zagged, avoiding another whining bullet that sizzled through the air beside his head. A full stride from his destination, he launched himself in a head-on leap over the trough. He hit the ground and rolled backward, pressing his length against the trough's wood.

From atop the seamstress shop a rifle fired. The force of the impact vibrated along the gambler's spine when the slug slammed into the trough. He heard ice crack and split as the bullet failed in its attempt to drive through the solid block of ice filling the trough.

A blur of movement at the corner of an eye, drew Chance's gaze upward. One of Ransons stood on the edge of the roof directly above. The rifleman's weapon pressed solidly against the hollow of his right shoulder.

With no thought of wasted ammunition, Chance wrenched his Remington high and fired. He missed his mark, but the unexpected shot was enough to ruin the aim of the man above when he jumped back. His spoiled shot spent itself in the middle of the street.

"You boys, stay back," Clay Ranson's voice called out. "No need gettin' yourselves kilt. He ain't goin' nowhere. Soon as he sticks his head out, Willie and Garr will pick him off."

That's the damned truth! Chance cursed to himself. Although the watering trough provided cover, his position remained tenuous at best. One false move and the Ransons perched atop the seamstress shop across the street would quickly put an end to one Chance Sharpe.

The gambler's gaze darted about in desperation. There was no place for him to go, except the seed and feed store. In spite of the CLOSED sign hanging on the door, he was more than willing to throw himself through the glass window to escape his would-be killers. However, it wasn't the windows that kept him from making a try for the store. It was the two steps that led from the street to the store front. The rifles across the street would easily find his back before he cleared the first step.

"I told you boys to stand back," Clay Ranson shouted again. "Now do like I say before you get yourselves shot!"

A scramble of retreating boots came from overhead as the two men above Chance followed orders.

The gambler cursed again. He hadn't even noticed the riflemen creeping forward to pick him off! He added another string of curses for his delay in buying a hat. Had one topped his head, he could have used the muzzle of his pistol to poke it above the rim of the trough and draw the fire of the two across the street. Their shots wasted, he could run for the seed and feed.

But you haven't got a damned hat! And wishing that you did isn't doing one bit of good! he reprimanded himself for wool gathering. Wishful thinking wasn't going to get him out of this. He had to think and think clearly.

"Chance!" The voice that called his name didn't belong to Clay Ranson. It was John Tolbert! "Chance, run for the jail. We'll cover you!"

Two rifles barked. Again feet scrambled above him in a hasty retreat. Four shots thundered in answer to the first two.

Chance didn't hesitate. He couldn't waste the precious seconds it would take for the rooftop riflemen to reload their expended weapons. Pushing to his feet, he ran westward toward the deputy and Frank Clancy standing outside the jail emptying their six-shooters at the Ransons, who pressed belly down on the roofs.

"In the jail, quick," Tolbert ordered as the gambler reached his side.

Chance offered no argument and shot inside the wooden building. Clancy and Tolbert followed at his heels, slamming the door closed behind them.

FIFTEEN

Chance looked at Tolbert and then Frank Clancy, grinning. "I never thought I'd ever say this, but I'm damned glad to see *you!*"

Clancy started to speak, only to be cut off by the deputy. "It's no time to go celebrating. You aren't a hell of a lot better off in here than you were outside. Take a gander across the street."

Tolbert opened the door a crack. The gambler peered out.

"What is it?" Clancy asked.

"Two men on the roof across the street," Chance answered, closing the door.

"See what it looks like out back, Frank," Tolbert ordered.

The man hastened through the door leading to the cells. He returned just as quickly. "They've pulled up a wagon in the back. Two men with rifles are inside."

"They don't want us going anywhere." The lawman glanced at Chance and shrugged. "I told you we didn't do you any favors bringing you in here."

"At least it's warm." The gambler walked beside the potbellied stove and held out his hands to chase away the cold.

"For a while," Tolbert replied with one of his irritating grunts. "Those ten logs are all the firewood we have. It won't take long to go through them."

"We can bust up the chairs and desk," Frank suggested.

"After that?" Chance asked, just beginning to realize their precarious situation.

"I don't know," Tolbert answered with a shake of his head. "I haven't thought that far ahead yet."

"Grand," the gambler replied with no attempt to hide his disgust. "Just grand!"

Chance opened the door wide enough to peer outside with one eye. The two riflemen still stood vigil on the roof across the street. "They haven't moved a muscle in three hours."

"Didn't expect that they'd just up and disappear," the deputy said from behind the office's desk. "Ransons don't give up easily. They know time's on their side. All they have to do is wait for us to make a move."

"Speaking of which," Chance said, "have you come up with any ideas yet?"

"I'm pondering one," Tolbert answered. "Like to hear what you two think."

"Does it matter?" the gambler asked.

"Nope." The deputy shook his head. "But you might see something I'm overlooking."

"We're listening," Frank said, tilting his head for the lawman to go on.

The deputy shifted in his chair, his gaze drifting over the ceiling. Chance glanced up; there was nothing there except a latched trap door that led to a crawl space between ceiling and roof, which Sheriff Glen Pardee had used to store his records. The gambler knew—he had asked earlier.

"The way I see it," Tolbert began. "We ain't got a chance if we remain here. If we're going to make it, we've got to get Martin to another town. One with a U.S. Marshal would be nice—maybe Fargo."

"We could wait until dark to make our move," Frank said eagerly. "If we make it to the livery stable, we could be saddled up and be gone a half hour or so before Clay Ranson ever knew we'd lit out."

The deputy nodded. "My thinking, exactly."

"Except you're both overlooking a major problem," the gambler broke in. "Ranson's men are guarding the front and back doors to this jail. We aren't setting a foot outside without them noticing."

"Haven't neglected that," Tolbert answered. "Just haven't come up with an answer to it yet. I was hoping one of you might have an idea or two."

Chance held his exasperation in check as he glanced back outside. The two riflemen held their weapons ready. "Wonder how many men the old man's got outside?"

"Why don't you walk over to the hotel and ask that singer you've been cuddled up with these past few days," Frank said, his voice seeped in sarcasm. "She was mighty cozy with at least one Ranson I know of before you come to town. Might be she's bundlin' with one right now."

Chance swirled on the man, his eyes narrowing to slits of angry steel blue. "You care to explain that?"

"Don't get riled." Tolbert stood and waved Frank away from the gambler. "He didn't mean nothing. Frank was just stating a fact."

"Fact?" Chance frowned.

"Marilee Dupree had been more than just a little friendly with Martin Ranson before I brought you into town," the deputy said. "I'm not saying that she was as friendly as she's been with you, but Martin took a shining to her, and I never noticed her doing anything to make him hesitate."

"Are you certain?" Chance tried to ignore the sinking feeling in the pit of his stomach. "She told me that she knew Martin, but just to speak with."

"They done more than speak," Frank spoke up again. "I seen 'em out at Rocky Run on Potter's Creek a couple times on warm fall afternoons. They had a blanket spread on the ground and one of them straw baskets with food. A man would have thought they was on some church picnic or something."

Rocky Run—Potter's Creek, the names were somehow familiar to Chance, but he couldn't pigeonhole them. Nor did he have time to ponder it. Footsteps drew his attention outside. He glanced out the cracked door. "A woman's crossing the street with a basket on her arm."

"A woman?" The deputy moved to the door and edged Chance aside. "It's Nellie from the café. She doesn't look like she wants to be here."

"John, John Tolbert, open up and let me in," the woman called out when she stopped in front of the jail.

Making certain everyone was clear, the lawman threw the door wide and held it until the woman entered. Tolbert had been right. The gray-haired, middle-aged Nellie looked frightened and bedraggled. Her wide eyes nervously darted around the jail office's interior.

"Nellie, what in damnation are you doing here?" Tolbert demanded.

"Don't you go cussing at me John Tolbert!" The café owner shoved the basket into the deputy's arms. "I wouldn't be here if it weren't for Clay Ranson. He forced me to come. Said I was to tell you that condemned men have a right to a last meal."

"Neighborly of him," Chance said without humor as he accepted the basket filled with fried chicken and biscuits from Tolbert. "At least we'll die with full bellies."

The deputy ignored the gambler. "Ranson say anything else?"

"Just to tell you that he had thirty men outside, and that there was no way any of you was getting away after you shot down his sons last night," the woman answered, her whole body atremble. "He said I was to bring you that, then get out. I brung it. Now I'm going. This is no place for an old lady."

Tolbert blocked her path to the door. "One more thing, Nellie. Is Ranson lying, or does he have that many men?"

"Maybe more—and all his kin. He's got them spread out all around town," she answered. "He means what he says, John. Even if you let Martin go, he intends to see you three dead."

The lawman nodded and opened the door. Nellie quickly exited and bustled down the street toward her café.

"Come up with an idea about getting us out of here tonight?" Chance asked while Tolbert relatched the door. The deputy shook his head. Chance took a deep breath and said, "Well, I have."

"You certain that you want to do this?" Tolbert asked as they moved to the jail's back door.

"Hell no, I don't want to do this," Chance replied. "But it won't work with either you or Frank. Both of you have too much at stake, and the Ransons damned well know it. I'm an unknown factor. They don't know what to expect from me."

The deputy nodded to Frank Clancy, who opened a cell and motioned Martin Ranson outside with a wave of a cocked Colt. Chance lifted high the oil lamp he held in his left hand. In spite of all the trouble Martin had caused him, this was the first time he had laid eyes on the young murderer.

And young he was. The gambler estimated his age at no more than twenty years. He stood an inch under six foot and sported a thick head of sandy brown hair. Except for a cruel twist to his lips, his features were clean and handsome.

"He's cuffed." Frank pushed the prisoner toward the gambler. "Just make damned sure he don't get away from you."

"If he does, I'm a dead man." Chance maneuvered Martin in front of him and pressed the Remington's barrel against the small of his back. "Make one wrong move—even a twitch of your head—and I'll pull the trigger."

Martin Ranson nodded.

The gambler glanced at Tolbert. "Open the door and say a prayer."

The deputy reached out and pulled the rear door open. Chance nudged Martin Ranson outside. Three strides beyond the threshold, he halted the young killer and raised the oil lamp over Martin's head to make certain the two waiting in the wagon saw who they faced. He watched two shadows rise from the wagon bed with rifles ready. Neither man fired.

"I want to make a trade," Chance said, with a prayer that his voice didn't carry beyond the wagon. "This ain't my fight. My life for the boy here and the two I've got tied up inside."

He felt Martin tense, but the young prisoner made no attempt to uncover his ruse. The gambler drew a breath to steady himself while he listened to the two shadowed men whisper between themselves.

"You say the others are tied up inside?" one of the men eventually questioned.

"Bound and gagged in one of the cells," Chance replied. He motioned Martin to one side with the Remington's guiding pressure. "Take a look for yourselves. I ain't going nowhere."

The two hesitated for another exchange of whispers, then stepped from the wagon. With their rifles on Chance, they backed toward the opened jail door. Neither of them saw Tolbert and Frank step out and drive rifle butts into the back of their heads. Both collapsed to the ground without a sound. While Frank and the deputy dragged the unconscious men into a cell, the gambler blew out the lamp and placed it on the ground.

"Open wide," Tolbert ordered his prisoner when he rejoined Chance. When Martin did, he stuffed a gag into his mouth. "Just to make sure that he doesn't try to give us away. Now, let's move out."

Cautiously, aware of unseen eyes that might follow them in the night, they worked behind the shops and buildings that lined Beltin's Main Street. Likewise, Tolbert swung them in a wide arc around the intersection of the town's two streets so that they approached Harrison Clive's livery stable from the rear and entered.

"Work quietly, but saddle up as fast as you can," the deputy ordered. "Sooner or later someone's going to check on those two we knocked out. I want us to be as far away from town as possible when they do."

"You ain't goin' nowhere, Deputy." Three shadows moved in the livery stable's darkness. "You done reached the end of your rope."

The flash of Tolbert's spitting Colt briefly illuminated the faces of three Ransons. Their pistols answered the shots. In turn Chance and Frank fired, emptying the chambers of their sixshooters.

The thunder of exploding gunpowder died and silence reigned. The three challengers lay dead.

"Chance, Frank?" the deputy questioned in the dark.

"Here," Chance replied.

"I'm still standin'," Frank answered.

"Good, 'cause I think Martin's been hit. Somebody find a light," Tolbert ordered.

Frank discovered a lantern and lit it with a match. Its light revealed a dark moist blossom of blood spreading across Martin's thigh as he lay on the ground, groaning. The lawman shook his head. "He's bleeding bad."

Neither Chance nor Frank had the opportunity to answer. Clay Ranson called from outside. "If anybody's still alive in there, you've got five minutes to come out with your hands high. After that, I'm going to burn this damned barn down!"

SIXTEEN

"You inside, did ya hear me?" Clay Ranson continued to shout. "You've got five minutes before me and the boys burn that barn down around your ears!"

Chance's gaze shot to John Tolbert. "I think that he's made himself perfectly clear."

"Perfectly!" The deputy grunted. His head twisted from side to side as though searching for an avenue of escape. There was none, only a livery stable filled with very inflammable hay and straw.

"Four minutes!" Ranson called out.

"What'll we do?" This from Frank Clancy, whose own eyes darted about the livery stable.

"He hasn't thought that far," the gambler said with sarcasm thick on his tongue.

Tolbert shot Chance a glare that was meant to kill. He then looked at the closed front doors to the livery stable. "We hear you, Clay. But I wouldn't be too hasty about tossing your torches in. You'll kill us, but you'll also barbecue Martin."

There was a moment of heavy silence, then Ranson shouted, "Martin? You in there, Martin?"

Tolbert yanked the gag from Martin's mouth. "Answer him."

The young killer sat on the floor, glaring defiantly at the lawman. "Answer him yourself. I'd just as well see you and your friends burn, Deputy."

"Be that as it may"—Tolbert's right foot slashed out, burying the pointed toe of his boot in Martin's wounded leg—"but I ain't got a hankering to die, at least not right now."

Martin howled, grasping his thigh. The deputy's toe prodded him again—harder. "I said *answer* him!"

"I'm in here, Pa," Martin conceded to the lawman's demands. "And I'm hurt, Pa!"

"Hurt?" Doubt crept into Clay Ranson's voice.

Tolbert stuffed the gag back into his prisoner's mouth before he could utter another sound. "That's right, Clay. Martin's hurt. One of your kin put a chunk of lead in his leg before we could stop them. He's bleeding like a stuck pig—probably dying. But he'll live long enough to feel the flames."

Chance glanced at the deputy and grinned his approval. Tolbert definitely had a style to be reckoned with.

Outside in barely discernable tones, Clay Ranson ordered his small army of men to extingiush their torches. *So far so good,* Chance sensed a thread of hope.

"All right, Deputy," the head of the Ranson clan shouted. "We've reached a Mexican standoff. Call your next move."

"Martin needs medical help," Tolbert answered. "You and your men back off and hold your guns. My deputies and I will take Martin to Doc Henry's to get him patched up."

"Deputies?" Chance arched an eyebrow in question. "I thought I was just some poor sucker who got dragged into this."

"I promoted you," the deputy replied. "I'll see you get a star to pin on your chest—if we ever get back to the jail."

"A comforting thought," the gambler replied in disgust.

"No tricks, Deputy?" Ranson shouted.

"No tricks," the lawman called. "You give us free passage to Doc's and then the jail, and I guarantee your son doesn't bleed to death."

Again silence hung in the air for several seconds before Ranson answered, "Me and my boys are backing away. Ain't nobody goin' to bother you none. Now get Martin to the Doc's."

"We'll wait three minutes, then move out." Tolbert tilted his head toward the barn's double doors as he glanced at his companions. "If there's any trouble, it's every man for himself."

"That's as good as I can do." Doc Henry tied off the bandage he wrapped around Martin's thigh. "The bleeding's stopped, but he's liable to tear open the stitches if you go and move him."

Tolbert helped his prisoner to his feet. "Ain't got no choice, Doc. Unless you'd like for us to make a stand in your house."

"Move him," the physician said without pause. "But remember I warned you about those stitches."

"We're warned." The deputy accepted a crutch and passed it to his prisoner. "Move it." While Martin hobbled toward the door, Tolbert glanced at Chance and Frank. "Stay in close. Clay won't try anything if there's a chance of hitting his son. Stray too wide, and he'll pick you off."

In a tight knot the three men moved Martin into the night and marched him down Main Street. Aware of the twenty-five pairs of Ranson eyes that focused on their every move, Tolbert kept to one side of the street in the hope that the night's shadows would confuse those who watched and keep their fingers off the triggers of their guns.

It was a plan that worked. The four men made it to the jail and opened the door before they had a hint of Ranson activity. The moment Frank checked the jail's interior,

Clay Ranson called out, "Deputy, before you go holing up like a rabbit, I've got a proposition for you."

Tolbert turned back to the dark street, using Martin as a shield from possible attack. "Let's hear it, Clay."

"You and your boys have fifteen minutes to set my son loose or I'm going to start killing the fine citizens of Beltin—one every five minutes," the patriarch of the Ranson clan shouted. "Starting with this pretty li'l thing."

A woman's whimper sounded from an alley. Two men stepped from the darkness. Between them they dragged—Marilee! Terror twisted the singer's face as her captors placed the muzzles of their pistols against her temples.

"Fifteen minutes, Deputy! Meet me at the center of town in fifteen minutes, and you can have the li'l lady in exchange for Martin. If you don't, I'll blow her brains out. Five minutes after that, Nellie'll die," Ranson repeated his terms as the two men tugged Marilee back into the alley. "Fifteen minutes, Deputy. No more, no less!"

Tolbert reached out, grabbed Martin's collar, and yanked him into the jail. Frank slammed the door closed.

"Damn!" Frustration welled in the lawman's voice. "That old bastard isn't fooling. He'll kill the girl and then every person in this town, unless he gets what he wants."

"Then he'll kill all of you." A smug smile spread over Martin's face.

And was immediately wiped away by a backhanded swipe from the deputy that sent his prisoner sprawling to the floor. "Another word out of you, and you won't last the fifteen minutes!"

Tolbert glared at his prisoner, leaving no doubt that he looked for an excuse to put another bullet in the young killer. Martin offered no further comment, but that smirk hung on his lips.

"What'r'ya goin' to do?" Frank asked, the barrel of his own rifle homed on Martin.

"Only one thing I can do." The lawman stiffened as he spoke. "I've got to give them Martin."

Chance breathed a sigh of relief. Marilee still might get out of this alive.

Following Tolbert's directions they walked down the middle of Main Street side by side. In front of them Martin limped on a single crutch.

Chance's gaze shifted from side to side. He sensed the Ransons staring on, but he was damned if he could see them slink back in the concealing shadows. *A fool's game,* the thought repeated in his mind. They were committing suicide, but Clay Ranson had given them no other choice.

"That's far enough," the deputy ordered when they reached the intersection of Beltin's two streets. He then called out, "All right, Clay. We're here. Bring out the girl!"

Ranson and two of his kin stepped from an alley on the opposite side of the intersection with Marilee proceeding them at gunpoint. They walked to the center of the street and halted. Clay took Marilee's arm and moved forward a stride. "We let them cross at the same time, Deputy."

"If there's any funny business, put a slug in Martin's back," Tolbert whispered to Frank, who nodded in answer, then to Clay, "Say when."

"Now." Ranson released Marilee's arm.

Together the lovely singer and the hobbling killer moved forward. Without a glance at each other, they passed at the center of the intersection. Chance's rifle lifted, ready for the slightest sign of trouble.

The gambler's left arm snaked to clasp around Marilee's waist the instant she was in reach. She hugged close, trembling, but had the sense not to speak.

"Back away," Tolbert whispered. "And keep your eyes open."

No other sound passed their lips while they backstepped down Main Street. On the opposite side of the intersection, Clay Ranson and his kin did the same.

The hairs on the back of Chance's neck prickled halfway to the jail. The night had swallowed the Ransons; they were no longer in sight. The unmistakable metallic click of a cocking hammer came from his right.

Tolbert apparently heard the same sound. "It's every man for himself!"

The deputy swung to his right, leveled his rifle in the direction of the clicking hammer, and fired. A man groaned above the din of the rifle shot.

Chance's own rifle spat fire and lead into a shadow that moved within the shadows to his right. As that shadow crumpled, he shoved Marilee toward the darkness of an alley, while he tossed away the now useless single-shot rifle to free the Remington from its holster.

The deadly bark of rifle and pistol filled the night. Fiery blossoms of blue and yellow flowered from both sides of the street as the concealed Ransons opened up.

The gambler emptied one chamber at a rifle-toting gunman who stood atop the Hotel Beltin and took aim. The man screamed when lead struck home. Doubling over, he tumbled head first from the roof to the ground below.

Chance didn't have time for a second shot; the hail of bullets that slammed into the snow around him couldn't be ignored. He spun and followed Marilee into the narrow alley.

"There's nowhere to go!" The singer moved to his side when he plunged into the shadows. "They're everywhere!"

With a quick glance to both sides to make certain no Ranson followed him, the gambler pointed to a crawl space beneath the seed and feed store on their left. "You're not going anywhere. Get under there and stay put until this is over. I don't want them using you again."

"Chance?" Marilee's brow furrowed in doubt, then she nodded in acceptance. Throwing her arms around him, she hugged him tightly and kissed his lips. "Be careful. I don't want to lose you again."

"My sentiments exactly," he answered, then urged her beneath the building.

When she was safely concealed he used the side of a boot to cover the traces of her movement left in the snow. Another quick glance behind him and the gambler moved to the rear of the narrow alley. There he pressed flat against the wall of the seed and feed and peered beyond. There was no movement.

Sucking down a steadying breath, he stepped from the alley and sprinted toward the back entrance of the jail a hundred yards from his position. He covered half the distance when two dark forms stepped from between two buildings. Before either of the men could level their pistols, Chance's Remington spoke—twice! The impact of the .44 caliber slugs threw them backward into the snow, where they died, clutching their chests. The gambler gave them no more than a passing glance as he continued toward the jail.

Reaching the wooden structure, he flattened himself against the wall and nudged the door open with an extended toe. The thunder of a rifle blasted from within. Thanking the fates for his caution, he pushed from the wall and stepped into the doorway, his six-shooter spitting fire. His second shot caught a bearded man in the forehead while he tried to free a pistol from his belt. Aside from the two Ransons still locked in their cell, the rest of the jail was empty.

Closing the rear door, Chance reloaded while he moved into the jail's office. Clicking the cylinder of the Remington closed, he threw open the front door. Tolbert and Frank ran a zigzagging path toward him. The gambler stepped out, raised the pistol, and provided what cover fire he could.

The deputy darted through the door first. Ten feet behind him Frank followed. One stride from the open doorway, he groaned and threw himself into the jail, both hands grabbing his left leg. Chance wasted no time emptying the last chamber of his revolver and following him inside.

SEVENTEEN

"How's that?" John Tolbert tied a makeshift bandage around Frank Clancy's left calf while Chance moved from the jail's back door to the front.

"I'm all right. The bullet went straight through my leg." Frank stood. "See? Everything's as good as new."

The gambler glanced at the man. Frank wasn't fooling anyone. He spoke through gritted teeth, his face was as pale as a bleached sheet, and sweat glistened on his forehead. The wounded leg would carry his weight for no more than a dozen steps—if that far.

"Sit back down, Frank. No need tiring yourself for nothing," the deputy said, watching the man gratefully sink into the chair. Tolbert turned to Chance. "What's it look like?"

"We're back to square one," Chance replied. "Ranson has men covering us outside both doors."

"It won't take him long to realize that we've still got two of his kin locked up," the lawman said. "Then it all begins again."

"We should have whittled them down a mite." This from Frank. "I know I hit at least two—maybe three."

"Counting the one I took in here," Chance said, "I shot four."

"Three here," Tolbert added. "That leaves twenty-one men Clay still—"

"Sixteen," the gambler corrected. "You're forgetting the two in the cell and the three we took at the livery stable."

"Seventeen," Tolbert replied with a shake of his head. "That's counting Martin. Although I don't think he's in any shape to do much fighting."

The deputy paused to glance around. He pursed his lips and released his breath in a loud gush of disgust. "Seventeen men or thirty—seems we're just splitting hairs. They've got us pinned down, and all we can do is wait for their next move."

"We can't wait," Chance said firmly. "We won't get out of this alive unless we make the next move."

Doubt wrinkled Tolbert's forehead when he looked at the gambler. "I think I'm missing something. I thought you said that the Ransons had us covered."

"Front and back," Chance said, then pointed to the ceiling. "But they aren't sitting on top of us?"

The lawman's frown of doubt remained on his face.

"Do you still have that buckhorn hunting knife that you took off of me?" When Tolbert nodded and pointed to the desk, Chance crossed the room and extracted the blade from a drawer. He then took a ladder from the corner, leaned it against the wall and climbed to the trap door in the ceiling.

"I told you that there's nothing but papers stored up there," Tolbert said when the gambler pushed into the ceiling crawl space.

"I know," Chance answered while he reached up and tested the roof that pressed down over his head. Three feet from the open trap door a weak board sagged beneath the weight of the snow sitting atop the jail. "But I also think that I've found another way out of here. I *could* use a hand up here."

The deputy scrambled up the ladder. A smile spread across his face when he saw the board that held the gambler's interest. Prying with the knife's blade and tugging with bare hands, they began to tear out the wood.

"This will stop the first man who tries to come through that door." Chance lightly touched the tautly stretched twine that ran from the shotgun's trigger to the handle of the front door. The shotgun, its twin barrels aimed at the door, was securely tied to the desk. "It's not another man, but it should give them pause if they decide to rush the jail."

"I've got another just like it rigged to the back door," Tolbert said as he stepped into the office through the door leading from the cells. "You certain that you can handle it alone here, Frank?"

"I'm not hurtin' on firepower." The man nodded to the four loaded revolvers and five rifles laying atop the desk. "I plan to sit myself down behind that desk and just wait. I figure I can stop anybody that gets passed those shotguns."

The lawman bit at his lip, then nodded. "Good luck."

"Same to you," Frank answered, then added. "And remember, don't try coming back in those doors without announcin' yourself. I'd hate for either of you to accidentally blow a hole in your middles."

"We'll remember that," Chance assured him, then moved to the ladder behind Tolbert.

"Deputy!" Clay Ranson hailed from outside. "Deputy, I know you got two of my cousins in there. I want them! It's the same deal as before. Turn 'em over, or I'll start killin' your good citizens."

The gambler and lawman froze halfway up the ladder. Their worse fears had been realized. In spite of their haste, they hadn't moved fast enough!

"Go right ahead and kill anyone you want, you old dried up son of a bitch!" It was Frank who answered Ranson. "You ain't dealing with Deputy Tolbert no more. Your boys saw to him real good—bullet right between the shoulders. Now you got Frank Clancy to haggle with, and I ain't so easy. You want these two? Give me Martin."

"Are you crazy?" Doubt twinged Ranson's voice. "I said I was going to start killin' citizens!"

"And I said go right ahead!" Frank shouted back. "That yellow-bellied son of yours killed my brother. Ain't a person in town gives a damn about Wesley's death, except me. Kill every one of the bastards for all I care. If you want these two I got, you're goin' have to give me Martin. That's the only deal I'm amakin'!"

Frank looked up and motioned his two companions up the ladder. "Go on and git! I've got the son of a bitch buffaloed. Go on with your business. He ain't goin' to stand outside and argue all night."

When Chance and the deputy disappeared into the ceiling, Frank called out again, "Oh! Clay Ranson, I forgot to mention somethin'. If I hear a shot from out there, I intend to start shooting pieces off these boys in here. An ear, a finger, a toe, a foot—it don't make me no never mind."

"Clancy, you're bluffing!" Clay shouted while Chance wiggled through the narrow hole he and Tolbert had opened in the roof. Flat on his stomach he crawled toward the front of the roof. Ranson stood in the shadows across the street.

"Bluffin' am I? I'll show you who the hell is bluffin'!" Frank answered. A second later a shot rang out, followed by a blood-curdling scream. "That was a finger, Ranson. Press me, and I'll take off his tallywacker with the next shot! Ain't doing him much good anyway!"

"Frank runs a good bluff," Chance whispered as Tolbert slipped beside him to survey the street.

"If he is bluffing," the deputy answered.

"All right, all right, Clancy. You win this round, but the fight's not over," Ranson conceded. While the gambler and deputy watched, the man disappeared down an alley beside the hotel.

"It's time to move while Frank's got their heads turned," Tolbert whispered. "Our best shot is to take them from behind."

"One at a time," Chance admended. "Shall we hit the two back of the jail first?"

"My thoughts exactly."

Twisting, the two belly-crawled to the right side of the roof and wiggled down to the roof of the building beside the jail. Two more roofs later they reached an alley. Two of Ranson's men waited below. Freeing hunting knives from their belts, Tolbert and the gambler rose to a crouch. With a nod they leaped below.

Chance's boots slammed directly atop his man's shoulders. He heard bones snap beneath the impact. Together they collapsed to the ground, the gambler's blade seeking and finding the man's throat before he could utter a warning. When he rose and turned, he saw the deputy hovering over the second man, whose life's blood flowed into the snow.

"That leaves fifteen." Chance moved to the back of the alley. He could barely discern the two riflemen crouched behind the wagon in back of the jail. "Those two will have to wait. There's no way to get at them without being seen."

The deputy's head poked out to take a look. "Afraid you're right. Let's move on to the next alley."

Clinging to the building's shadows, Chance slipped from the alley. Step by cautious step he moved, his temples apounding, his mouth dry, and his palms sweating. Five buildings down, he crouched at the entrance to the next alley and peered into it. One man clutching a rifle stood watching the street.

Chance held up a hand to halt Tolbert, then signaled him with one finger to indicate the sole man within the alley. The gambler then reached into the snow and compressed a ball with his fist. Leaning forward again, he estimated twenty-five feet from the front of the alley to his position. *Ten cautious strides.* He tossed the snowball against the wall across from him, then ducked back.

Within the alley, the man swung around. Snow crunched beneath his boots as he edged toward the end of the alleyway.

Eight . . . nine . . . Chance counted each of the man's footfalls. On ten, he leaped up. With his left hand he knocked the guard's rifle muzzle aside, and with his right, he drove the length of the hunting knife into the man's heart.

"Fourteen," Tolbert subtracted another from the men they still faced while he stepped over the twitching corpse and edged to the front of the alley.

Chance joined him, scanning the empty street. Except for the two men perched on the roof across from the jail, he failed to locate any of the Ransons. A tiny flare of red pulled his eyes to the dark interior of Nellie's Café. He nudged the deputy. "They're in there. I can see them smoking."

"Three smokes," the lawman counted the cherry red auras of burning tobacco visible behind the café's window. "Wonder how many are holed up inside?"

"The more the merrier," Chance answered. "Makes it a damned site easier than tracking them down one at a time."

Before Tolbert answered, the door to the café opened. A man stepped out, glanced up and down the street, then crossed on a direct line for the alley.

"Get back," Chance said, lifting the hunting knife. "I'll handle this."

The lawman didn't protest. Sinking back, he moved to the rear of the alley. Chance's attention homed on the Ranson who walked toward him.

"Herschel," the man said when he joined the gambler in the shadows, "Clay wants you over in the café. He's got an idea how to get at that crazy bastard in the ja—uuggaahhh!"

The man died with his sentence hanging on his tongue as Chance slipped the steel blade between his ribs and twisted. With a hand clamped over his mouth to muffle his last gasps, the gambler followed his slumping body to the ground. Only when the last twitch passed from his muscles did he release his hold and wave Tolbert back to him.

"Clay Ranson is in the café," Chance said. "If we can get to him, we've a slim chance of pulling this off."

"We can't simply walk in there," Tolbert answered.

"That's exactly what I intend to do. Strip off his coat and hat," the gambler ordered, then stepped back to the first man who had died in the alley and took his coat and hat. Seconds later he stood wearing the man's clothing. "In the dark, nobody's going to notice who we are until it's too late."

Tolbert grinned, the seed of Chance's plan sinking into his head. He exchanged his own coat and hat for those in his hands. "You're as crazy as a horse that's been eating loco weed, Chance. But I like the way you think. We both walk in the front door—they'll never expect us."

"*I* walk in the front," the gambler corrected. "You're going to come in the back of the café."

"Even better." The deputy glanced back to the street. "Give me five minutes to work my way into position."

"Five minutes." Chance nodded.

Tugging his borrowed hat low to his face, Tolbert stepped from the alley. For a moment he stood there as though surveying the situation, then he casually walked across the street. He disappeared down an alley three buildings from the café.

In a one-and-a-two rhythm, Chance counted the seconds. When he reached three hundred, he imitated the lawman and pulled the hat brim close to his face. He drew a long breath to quell the race of his heart and strode onto the street.

Crazy is right, he thought while each step brought him closer to the café's door. Only a man with half his wits about him would have ever considered such lunacy. It took the fool of fools to carry it out. *That's what I am—the fool of fools!*

His mouth was filled with cotton by the time he reached the two steps that led to the café's front door. It took two additional deep breaths before he worked up the courage to move up the steps and open that door.

" 'Bout time you got here, Herschel."

Clay Ranson sat at a table just inside the café. Martin and two other men were with him. Five others sat at the table beside them. Chance silently thanked the darkness for cloaking his face.

"Billy found you a li'l something in the general store. It's in that chair there," Ranson said. "Reckon how you could set that outside the jail door?"

The gambler glanced to his right. A keg of gunpowder with a coil of fuse resting on its top sat in the chair. Chance's pounding heart tripled its wild pace.

"What'd'ya think, Herschel? That should take out the jail's office without touchin' the cells, shouldn't it?" Ranson asked.

"I think that I like this right where it is!" Chance freed his Remington and pressed the cocked revolver to the powder keg. "Everybody stay right where you are. I've got a nervous trigger finger."

"That's not Herschel!" This from Martin. "It's that gambler who threw in with Tolbert!"

"Can't say he's not smart." The deputy pushed into the café from the kitchen at the mention of his name.

Clay Ranson's head jerked around. "You ain't getting away with this!" His narrowed eyes shot back to the gambler. "You ain't goin' to pull that trigger. You do, and you'll die, too."

"The way you've laid things out, I'm going to die anyway." Chance shrugged. "Might as well take all of you with me."

Hate writhed on Ranson's face. He had reached a standoff and knew it. Chance had seen that same expression a hundred times on the faces of men across a poker table. A man either accepted defeat or he acted. Clay Ranson acted!

The slight quiver of his right arm gave him away. He went for his gun beneath the table! Chance didn't hesitate; he swung the Remington around and fired. That single shot opened a dark hole between Ranson's eyes. The man's head jerked back, his body following. He spilled to the café's floor a dead man. There was nothing else; dying was a simple act.

Chance's six-shooter jerked to cover a man who moved at the second table. "Try it, and you'll end up just like him."

The man placed his hands on the table in plain sight, as did the others with him.

"Each one of you reach down with two fingers and drop your pistols to the floor," Tolbert ordered.

One by one the men complied. They stood when the deputy told them to rise, then marched outside. With a muzzle pressed firmly to his temple, Martin called the remainder of his blood-thirsty relatives out into the street. Like the others, they tossed down their weapons and marched quietly toward the jail.

It took a few minutes for Frank to disable the shotgun inside, but once the twine was removed he held the cocked shattergun on the line of prisoners Tolbert and Chance marched into the waiting cells.

EIGHTEEN

Dawn found Chance and John Tolbert making their fourth sweep of Beltin. Shop by shop, alley by alley, and even climbing to an occasional rooftop to survey the Dakota Territory town, they methodically searched for any Ranson who might have stubbornly held out in the hope of avenging themselves and freeing their kin who now sat locked behind bars.

The Ransons they found were frozen corpses in the snow, their lives lost to hot lead or cold steel. These they grabbed by their boot heels and dragged out into the street. Later their board-stiff bodies would be collected by the undertaker to be claimed by their families or shoveled beneath the ground at a five-dollar-a-head cost to the town.

Chance ignored the grisly row of death-contorted bodies lining the street as he wearily trod toward the jail at the deputy's side. He preferred to focus his thoughts on the golden light of the morning. It heralded the coming of a new day; the bodies were a reminder of a nightmare-laden night that belonged to the past.

Outside the jail, the two men paused to scan Beltin's Main Street one last time. Here and there the town showed signs of awakening. A farmer sitting atop a flatbed wagon carrying wooden pails aslosh with steaming fresh milk urged a team of two mules through the snow. Merchants bustled in the cold, hastening to their shops.

Children ran laughing and shouting in answer to the clanking ring of a hand-held school bell.

They all look as though nothing has happened, the gambler sadly thought. Now and then he saw a passing man or woman cast a disdainful glance at the rigid reminders of the hell that had reigned in their town last night. Then their eyes would dart away as though they had merely glimpsed heaps of trash that had been cast into the street.

Chance glanced at the deputy. Tolbert lifted his eyebrows, sucked at his teeth, and shook his head, as though saying that he had no more idea of what to make of the scene than did the gambler.

Chance looked back to the town. Time would reveal how Beltin dealt with what had transpired in its streets last night. Perhaps the hours of terror would be shamefully hushed away, mentioned only in quick whispers with furtive glances to assure no one noticed the breach of good taste. Or it might be blown to the heroic proportions of cheap, pulp fiction. Either way, it would be a lie that hid the simple truth that three men had fought for their lives last night and survived to watch the rising sun of a new day. Beyond that, there was nothing else.

"Ever noticed how the air's always the coldest just at dawn?" Tolbert stared at the blazing orb that pushed above the horizon. He then looked at the gambler and shivered. "No need for us standing out here freezing to death when there's a fire inside."

Chance nodded and waved the lawman through the door ahead of him. Frank Clancy perched on the edge of the office's desk with his left pants leg ripped open from ankle to knee. Doc Henry sat in a chair, wrapping a white bandage about his calf.

"How is it, Doc?" Tolbert asked while he deposited his rifle in a wall rack.

"It's as clean as a man could want." The physician tied off the bandage and stood. He looked at Frank. "Stay off of it as much as possible the next few days, and you'll save yourself some misery."

"What about the prisoners?" The deputy walked to the potbellied stove and poured two tin cups of coffee from a steaming pot atop it. He handed one to the gambler.

"Three of them have arm and shoulder wounds that I'll have to keep an eye on," Doc Henry replied while he closed his black bag and pulled on his coat. "I'll drop back in this evening."

Tolbert nodded and watched the physician leave before he sank into a chair and leaned back to stare at the ceiling. "Going to have to do something about the roof today. Wouldn't do to have snow coming through the hole we made."

Chance found a chair and dragged it beside the stove. He was too tired for idle conversation. It took what little energy remaining in his body to lift the mug to his lips and sip at the scalding hot coffee.

"If I wasn't so damned sleepy, I'd drag myself home and crawl into bed." Frank stretched out atop the desk, crossing his arms beneath his head as a pillow. "And if this wood wasn't so damned hard, I'd pass out right here."

"I need to get a wire off to Fargo as soon as the telegraph office opens," Tolbert said more to himself than his companions. "Hearing about the situation here might set a fire under one of those marshals and hurry him along to collect these prisoners. I sure as hell ain't got room for them in the jail. After I get the wire off, I'll think about sleeping."

Chance's thoughts briefly returned to his journey eastward. It would have to wait, at least for another day. "As soon as I finish this coffee, I intended to climb into one of the hotel's beds and sleep for the next day or twelve."

"I wouldn't do much sleeping if I had a woman waiting for me like the one waiting for you." There was no trace of malice or venom in Frank's tone.

Marilee. The lovely singer edged into the gambler's mind. He hadn't seen her since she had crawled beneath the seed and feed to escape the Ransons' bullets. He had checked on her during their first sweep of the town, but she had already abandoned her hiding place. *Back to the warmth of her hotel room and bed,* Chance thought with a smile. It would be good to join her.

"You think Martin will ever come loose with where he hid the bank money?" Frank rolled to his side to face the deputy.

Tolbert sipped at his coffee and leaned forward. "Don't know. His tongue might loosen a bit now that he knows his pa isn't going to get him out of this one. A lot of folks would breathe easier if he did. If he doesn't, it's going to be a long, cold winter."

The lawman took another swallow from his tin cup. "Speaking of money—the town of Beltin owes both of you five dollars in deputy pay for last night. I can pay you now out of the petty cash box in the desk."

"Keep your money." Chance stood and drained his coffee. "Five dollars for what I went through would be an insult. In the first place you never gave us those badges to wear. In the second place, I've got all I need to get back to the river."

The gambler's heart missed a beat when he shoved his hand into his coat pocket. All his fingers felt was leather!

"What's ailing you?" Frank pushed to an elbow. "You look like you just seen a ghost."

"I think I did—one from my past!" Chance pulled out his hand and stared at the empty palm. "I had three hundred dollars in this pocket. Now it's gone!"

"That's a hefty chunk of ailment. It would cause me to go pale, too," Frank said with a surprised whistle.

"Think you dropped it during the night?" Tolbert sat straight in his chair.

Chance's mind raced and his heart pounded. "We would have noticed three hundred dollars laying in the snow as many times as we've been over this town. No, I didn't lose it. A songbird took it—a very dangerous songbird!"

Just how dangerous he had forgotten these past few days! Chance groaned aloud as he recalled the hug and kiss Marilee had given him before she ducked beneath the seed and feed store last night. The hasty embrace provided ample time for quick fingers to dip into his pocket and liberate the three hundred that had nested there.

"Songbird?" Frank's face wrinkled in confusion. "What's he babblin' about?"

"Chance? What *are* you talking about?" Tolbert pressed.

"Marilee—dammit! She picked my pocket last night! I was so damned worried about the Ransons that I never noticed . . ." Chance's thoughts stumbled. "Wait just a minute!"

Three hundred dollars wasn't enough to get Marilee to California. She had said that she needed a thousand. Even with the hundred she had tucked away in the envelope behind the mirror, that only totaled four hundred—six hundred shy of her goal. Nor would she have gone for his three hundred unless she thought that he was going to die last night.

"Only she wasn't shy of the thousand," he said aloud. "Damn! Why didn't I see it before?" The gambler slapped a frustrated palm to his forehead.

"Chance?" There was worry in the deputy's voice. "Chance, are you all right?"

"Hell, no, I'm not all right. Are you as blind as me? Don't you see where your bank money is? Where it's been all the time?" Chance stared at the lawman. "It's been in this town. Martin Ranson never took it beyond the Hotel Beltin!"

Tolbert's eyes widened and his jaw sagged. "Your songbird!"

"Exactly!" Chance pivoted and left the jail in a dead run for the hotel. The deputy followed two strides behind.

Inside they shot past the clerk and darted up the stairs two at a time. A knock on Marilee's door brought no answer. The second rap on the door came from Tolbert's shoulder; the lock splintered and the door swung open on an empty room.

"She's gone." The deputy stared vacantly into the room.

"You have a gift for stating the obvious."

Chance pushed past him to throw open Marilee's closet. The clothes inside dangled from their hangers in various states of disarray. The blond had been in a hurry, grabbing what she could take in a short time, leaving the rest. *Probably stuffed into one valise,* he thought, recalling her escape from the *Wild Card.*

Tolbert dragged a small trunk from beneath the bed and opened it. "You better take a look at this."

Neatly stacked bank notes lined its bottom!

Atop the money lay a folded piece of paper that the deputy lifted and opened. "This is for you." He handed the paper to the gambler.

An all too familiar flow of graceful letters filled the page. A sickening lurch twisted the gambler's gut when he began to read.

Chance,

If you are reading this, you somehow lived through the night. I could not be certain of that and was forced to take matters in my own hands.

I have taken only the sum that I required from the money Martin stole and hid in my room. Your three hundred dollars will provide a cushion against unforeseen events.

Chance, if you truly wish to be with me, then you know where you can find me. I will be waiting for you.

"All of it's here, except for nine hundred dollars," Tolbert announced as Chance read the last line of Marilee's note—*Please understand and forgive me.*

"I know." The gambler handed the note back to the deputy.

Tolbert quickly read the message, then looked at his companion. "Do you know where she's headed?"

"California," Chance answered, his stomach tying itself in a taut knot.

"Don't see how it would do much good for us to give chase. She's got a good twelve hours' start on us," the deputy said as he closed the trunk. "I'll wire out her description to other lawmen in the area, but I doubt that it will do much good. This is a big country. A man, or a woman, can lose themselves in it if they're a mind."

Chance nodded and slipped his hands into his empty pockets. When he turned to Tolbert, it was to ask: "Did you mention something about owing me five dollars in deputy pay?"

Chance worked the stub of his last cigar between his teeth. He had busied the remnants of the stogie all afternoon while he played hand after hand of poker in the Golden Eagle Saloon. Luck rode on his shoulder; his five-dollar deputy's fee had swelled to a grand sum of ten dollars.

Better than losing, he reprimanded himself for his bitterness. He had worked fifteen dollars into three hundred once, he could do the same with the ten. *Even if it takes the whole damned winter!*

"Chance," John Tolbert's voice called to the gambler. Chance glanced over his shoulder. The deputy, who stood at the bar, held up a yellow sheet of paper. "Can you excuse yourself from the game a moment? This just arrived for you."

Doing just that, Chance walked to the lawman, who handed him the paper and said, "It's a telegram from New Orleans."

The message from Philip Duwayne explained the attorney's delay in answering Chance's wire. Philip had been in Baton Rouge when the telegram arrived. In brief sentences, the young lawyer mentioned a celebration aboard *Wild Card* when his friends and crew learned that he still lived. Attached to the telegram was a draft for two thousand dollars, which Philip had sent "in case you've been caught short." Thoughts of transforming ten dollars into three hundred evaporated from the gambler's mind.

"The bank can handle that check now," Tolbert said with a smile. "You might drop in before they close this evening."

"The same thought had crossed my mind," Chance answered, feeling as though the weight of the world had been lifted from his shoulders. He started for the saloon's doors, then halted and turned back to the deputy. "Did you send out those wires about Marilee yet?"

"Haven't gotten around to it. Too many other things have occupied my mind today." Tolbert shook his head.

"If another nine hundred dollars suddenly appeared, could you forget those telegrams?" Chance suggested.

The lawman thoughtfully rubbed a hand over his chin, then finally nodded. "I think that can be arranged. But are you certain you want to do that?"

It was Chance's turn to pause and ponder. "Not certain at all, but I'm going to do it anyway. Call it a way of keeping a promise."

Tolbert didn't understand, but Chance didn't care. He had promised Marilee the money. He was making certain she got it.

"What about you?" the deputy asked.

"As soon as I cash this check and place nine hundred in your hands, I intend to buy a mount and tack from Harrison Clive. Then after a good night's sleep, I'm going to ride out of this lovely town of yours tomorrow morning," the gambler answered.

Tolbert raised a questioning eyebrow. "Heading for California?"

"No." Chance shook his head. "No, my life's on the Mississippi and not in California." He walked to the saloon's doors and opened them before glancing back at the deputy and grinning. "But I might have to visit California one day."